PARTITIONS

"Amit Majmudar's exceptional debut brilliantly captures India at its most turbulent . . . A dazzling narrative."   *The Daily Mail*

"A greatly human dramatization of the persecution each religious group experienced at the hands of the others . . . Poignant but never maudlin."

Booklist, starred review

"Magnificent . . . Written with piercing beauty, alive with moral passion and sorrowful insight—a rueful masterpiece."   *Kirkus*, starred review

"Ambitious and impressive . . . [an] accomplished and praiseworthy novel" ****

New Internationalist

"[A] superb fiction debut . . . This novel will make you angry and sad, as it should; it will also leave you with a heightened sense of sympathy and hope for the people on both sides of an arbitrary border."   *The Wall Street Journal*

"Vivid."   *Metro*

"Unforgettable."   *The Boston Globe*

"Heart-wrenching."   *New York Post*

"Shimmering prose . . . and a poignant surprise ending."   *The Seattle Times*

PARTITIONS

Amit Majmudar

ONEWORLD

A Oneworld Book

First published by Oneworld Publications 2011
This paperback edition published in 2012

Copyright © Amit Majmudar 2011

The moral right of Amit Majmudar to be identified as the
Author of this work has been asserted by him in
accordance with the Copyright, Designs and Patents Act 1988

ISBN 978–1–85168–831–9 (Hardback)
ISBN 978–1–85168–840–1 (Paperback)
ISBN 978–1–85168–785–5 (eBook)

Typeset by Jayvee, Trivandrum, India
Cover design by vaguleymemorable.com
Printed and bound in Great Britain by
CPI Group (UK) Ltd, Croydon, CR0 4YY

Oneworld Publications
185 Banbury Road
Oxford OX2 7AR
England

Learn more about Oneworld. Join our mailing list to
find out about our latest titles and special offers at:

www.oneworld-publications.com

Leave India to God.
—M. K. Gandhi, May 1942

This is the sadhu. He is standing in a river. The water is moving, but the reflection he casts is still. His legs are thin enough to be a crane's. Like a crane's, his identity switches between the reflection and the body. He doesn't think of either one as home. His hand clutches the ragged saffron high, under the water his ankles like a child's wrists. He tucks the dhoti tight for bath and prayer.

Look closer. The river is sinking underground. It leaves him standing in a swathe of dust. A grain of rice falls from his tilak like a fossilized pupa. The red of the tilak scabs and flakes from his forehead. The saffron dhoti bleeds white.

The earth has shifted, too. He isn't facing the sun any more. The sun hangs skewed to him, off to the side. It has wandered away from his morning ritual.

The scene is still changing. A new river lays itself under him. Train tracks. On the tracks, trains. On the trains, people and their possessions. White turbans in a row, bowed in exhaustion. Long staffs that once clicked wealths of cattle out to graze. Lumpy bundles in widow-white sarees, knotted at the top.

The trains are snippets of river, in motion even as they stand here in the station, drowning, taking on people as if taking on water. Every living body is a tiny collection of flow. Blood, lymph, ions, breath. The trains are standing, but the sadhu knows the stillness is illusory. A river sweeps the trains, and everyone in them and on them, down and under. The outriders lock fists on the rust-pocked metal of the handrails. The children are stowed in baggage-niches, chins to knees, heels to buttocks, wrists to shoulders—everything that can bend, bent. The women hold their sarees across their faces to protect against the pestilence of gazes. The sadhu, too, is here, reborn in the body of a nameless villager torn up by the roots and planted on the steel roof of a train, staring motionless at three smudges of motionless black smoke in the distance.

They are all in the river. The year is 1947. The river is heading for the falls.

· One ·

Connections

· One ·
_____

Connections

I know only three people in this infinitude. Two boys: one in a dark blue kurta with tiny golden beads embroidered around the collar, the other in a bright green one with silver beads, matching. Keshav is wearing the blue, Shankar the green. These are their favourite colours and these their best, most precious clothes, worn only twice, both times to weddings in Lahore.

I know these boys and the woman whose hands they are holding. A few hours ago, when the stray dogs took up a brittle, pulse-steady barking throughout the city, she gave the boys the choice, the trunk thrown open on the cot. The clothes they wore were the only clothes they could take. They didn't hesitate, and she didn't protest, simply tugged off their shirts and dropped the silk over their still-raised arms. It didn't occur to her that they might attract attention, that people might think she carries more than just a little barrel of hundred-rupee notes stuffed in her bodice. It doesn't matter. The dust of the journey will make sure the clothes don't attract attention for long. Besides, she wanted to give them this choice, this exercise of will. A small defiance to tide them over during the coming helplessness.

I know that cot, too, where the trunk still lies open. Its canvas rectangle. Two shawls and three blankets, and still I shivered on it.

There is no way she can manage even a small trunk. What with both boys to hold, she will need her hands free. All she carries are the rupees. Not even the lingam from the temple in the bedroom corner. They have to leave. This is Pakistan now. The land meant to be 'pak', pure. Pure of them. She knows the train is going to Delhi, and Delhi is better than where they are, but she has no one in Delhi, or anywhere. That is part of why I love her, that quality of being found, of having no origin. Portuguese missionaries had discovered her sleeping naked in a furrow, her body strangely scarred, no language on her tongue. Neither Muslim nor Hindu nor Sikh: some fourth natural creature sprung from the soil. All she had was me. So young, and still their teachings never really took. She swept the church and prayed where she was pointed. She was fifteen years old when I strolled past her and stopped and, trembling, put on my spectacles. The immense church bell was swinging over our heads. I found her, she found me. I had been alone eleven years by then, a widower, on good terms with my family and my late wife's, prosperous in my father's practice (I hadn't even got a new nameplate; his name was still over the office door). All until my second, shameful, marriage to a girl without family, without caste.

That woman is my wife, and those boys are my twins. Was my wife; were my twins. I am no longer with them. They lost me when the boys were a year and a half. But if I had a throat, and breath to push through that throat, and vocal cords to pinch close and shirr, I know what I would say.

I am here.

I am here because I am everywhere. I say I know only three people on the platform and in the trains, but in a sense I know all of them.

PARTITIONS

In a passenger compartment, a woman is peeling an orange into a handkerchief. All this desperation around her, but she and hers are safely aboard, and tiny drops of juice spray as the rind rips off white, tenaciously fibrous. Through the smell of urine and smoke and stale metal and sweat comes this wayward note of orange. In this suffocation of bodies, it smells like an open field and wind. All the faces turn to the glow in her lap. Mine does, too.

I dwell in that woman's eyes for a while. I rest there and use her calm to collect myself, though I cannot taste the orange with her. A sandal interrupts my meditation, braced on the bars across the open window. The foot is dusty, its big toenail black and still throbbing from something dropped during the frantic move. The sandal pauses and angles slightly as the man's weight is placed on it. A crust of dried mud flakes off into the train. It's an unexpected sight to see a foot like that, at face level, but the usual relationships among bodies do not hold any more, underwater as we are. I slide through the window, outside again. All down the train, people are clambering from the platform directly on to the train roof. Sandals open off their feet and close again, soles worn thin, dark, smooth at the heel. Like the dark sinkholes of shadow around their eyes. When they look down, I can't see their eyes at all. All I see are holes in a skull.

A man on the roof waves for a clearing. No one moves. Once his brother forces his way up, though, accommodation is made. Bodies squeezed tight squeeze tighter, fine adjustments of the buttocks and tugs of bundles, half-inch shuffles and scoots. Space forms where no space was. Below, two more brothers have lifted a makeshift carriage, a wooden plank around which the corners of a torn green saree have been knotted. A figure entirely swallowed in it swings gently. You see only the small curve of the back. The brothers grab the plank ends and lift this delicate human cargo safely on to the roof. The plank is set down and the knots picked free.

The people around them expected a pregnant girl or crippled child. It turns out to be their grandfather, toothless, three days unshaven, staring at the sky through sky-coloured cataracts. No movement, and for a while no blink. The others stare. They are looking for life. Still no blink. Finally the mouth closes. The throat rises and falls. The mouth opens. The people are satisfied; to have made room for the dying is tolerable. Just not for the dead.

I turn. A child is crying atop luggage stacked six high, set there as if to mark these goods claimed. He cannot get down. So many people, but he is on an island. I am the only one who hears the siren of his loneliness. I cannot comfort him. I may be everywhere, but I, too, don't know where his family is. In places such as these, I am almost blind. Shapes of bodies smear through time and overlap. I can trace glowing, individual strands only outside the station. An occasional pensive still life delineates itself, like a figure posing for a daguerreotype against a moving train—the place where a body has paused long enough to despair, or sleep, or hold a wound.

Only a fraction of my attention roams among the strangers at the station. I stay close to my wife and boys because I know what is going to happen here. This far ahead, at least, I can see. Not all the way to the end, because the end is never promised. But I can sense the danger a few minutes in advance, the way animals sense earthquakes, and I need to be here for it. Not that I can keep those tiny hands in hers or elbow apart this crowd before it panics. I cannot make space for them because I occupy none myself. Already the undertow exerts itself, invisible in these human waters but strong: rumour.

This will be the last train out. The tracks have been ripped up west of here. There are no more trains.

I cannot pinpoint where it starts. The idea springs up all around me at once, a hundred staccato thoughts and impressions. Rage at the sight of someone's back. *This is the last chance. Move. Let us on.* A bony hand clutches a rail. Elbows dig along a shoulder blade or spine. *This is the last one.* Shoulders brace low and slam a stranger's side or back. A woman screams. *The Mussulmaans are going to find us and hack us apart.* A turban is slapped on to the tracks. It unrolls under the train, an unbearable outrage. *You know what they did in Rawalpindi. It's going to happen here.*

Steam hisses. Shouts, everywhere. Inside the compartments, on the train car roofs. Loudest of all on the platform, where a tidal surge of bodies flattens chests against the steel, and more bodies drive themselves up the clogged steps.

Get on. Get out of the way. Move.

They are only a few steps from boarding when the panic and crush begins. The boys feel her yank them forwards. The force of surrounding bodies as much as her embrace holds them flush, their faces almost in her neck. Shankar and Keshav cling with both arms and legs. They are older now, boys, and her body is almost hidden under them. She is slight but she is strong. Her head is low. She uses the pushing behind her to weave through and up. She gets a foot on a step, loses it, gets it again and turns. A smaller child is handed bodily over their heads into the compartment, floating above the panic. He looks around curiously from his elevation. Relatives receive him inside. *My boys deserve that*, she thinks. They do. They deserve to float above this into familiar hands. She cannot get through the entry with the boys at her sides, so she slides them forwards and releases them. They want to help. Shankar pushes off the rail beside the entry, his hand feeling someone else's knuckles. Keshav pulls on the nearest shoulder for leverage, as if it were something inanimate. Another hiss. The train inches to the left. She has both feet on the steps. For a moment they are out of her arms, for a moment she has a feeling of liberation and future. She will hang here the whole journey if she has to, her boys on her neck.

This is when a hand I cannot slap down, whose fingers I cannot break, grabs her braid and pulls. Her head jerks back, and her body lifts.

Keshav shouts. The crowd closes over. The boys are submerged. They swim up again and see the narrow rectangle of platform has shifted. A new and unfamiliar crowd fights to board the quickening train. They are the only ones trying to get off. This is just as hard as trying to get on, maybe harder. They clamber on shifting shoulders. The people are packed that thick. The platform moves more quickly. Soon there will be dust and bare tracks. They do not have to speak to communicate what to do. The men who are hit or accidentally kicked by my boys shout and twist their faces as if this were the unacceptable outrage of the day. Finally, my boys approach the open air.

PARTITIONS

What happens next happens clumsily. They force themselves downwards, pushing off the ceiling, and a few of the outriders shout and squeeze aside to let them through—to resist would be to risk being pushed off. The boys are small but wiry, full of frantic energy and hard boy bones. If the platform had been three feet longer, both might have landed with a few deep scrapes, but the platform vanishes just as they make it out. Keshav just makes it: forearms, stomach and right cheek scraped, and a cut on his scalp. Shankar, though, falls just a second later. He clips the platform on his way down, and it flips him bodily. He hits the tracks, tumbles and skids a few feet, and comes to a stop in the train's monstrous shadow. The sun flashes between the cars.

The instant they fall, I sense another fall, this one gentler, on the other side of the new border. Doctor Ibrahim Masud. He is tall and thin, his chest, in his slept-in white undershirt, no broader than a boy's. Half his face is covered in shaving cream. The other half is freshly shaven, the razor drawn down the cheek, swished in the basin, tapped, brought up again.

I go back and see the way his fingers flared off the razor as it approached his skin. Thumb and forefinger took over for the delicate work. His earlobes dripped, and still drip, from the wake-up splashes that preceded the shave. Half his face finished, he sniffed the air, called the name Dara ji twice, and, hearing no answer from his servant, investigated. The rooms were hazy. (For Masud to notice smoke, it would have to fill the house; he tends not to sense his environment, his attention a flashlight, not a lamp.) *Something*, he thought, *must be burning in the street*. Trash was usually burned at dusk to disperse mosquitoes, or at dawn to warm hands. This hour, eight in the morning, was wrong. Two milk bottles, on the steps beside his shoes, had not been taken in. He wandered on to the stones barefoot, bewildered.

Hot wind, as though a furnace had swung open. Ash flecks flitted on to his raised wrist. He heard a crack and looked up.

Now, backing away from his house through its cast-iron front gate, he trips on his own feet. He hits the ground at the same instant my twins, hundreds of miles west of him, land on the tracks.

Get up, boys. Get up.

Car after car sways past Shankar, brisk now. Face-like masks see him and assume he is dead—a feature of the landscape, indifferent, plant-like. Keshav, bleeding, pushes himself off the platform to retrieve his brother. To many, the sight of the boys brings up a surge of relief and gratitude—this is the kind of horror they are escaping. Then the train is gone, its rocking soft in the distance. Daylight again, and the uproar on the platform.

I feel Shankar's three broken ribs and the cut on Keshav's head. I marvel that Shankar's collarbone hasn't broken where he hit the edge of the platform. They cannot feel my hands. How will they travel? I have foreseen their courses, but I never saw these details, never knew they would be in pain, Shankar stabbed by every breath, Keshav's skin grated raw, no gauze, no plaster.

With Keshav's help, Shankar gets up, holding the side where he has broken his ribs. The pain is the worst he has felt since the time he sprained his ankle last year, but he is not crying. If he saw his mother, he would start; there would be someone to cry to. Right now he and Keshav are too scared. They hold each other, saying nothing as they look for a way back on to the platform. Keshav blinks and tastes his own blood. Shankar, seeing the cut on Keshav's scalp and the hair wet over it, daubs his brother's face with his sleeve. The pain doesn't stop him. It is an older brother's gesture, though he is actually only a minute older. An older brother's gesture, or a father's. The silk soaks dark.

Their faces are identical, but their bodies aren't. Shankar grows into Keshav's hand-me-downs. Other kids tease Keshav about stealing his brother's food, even though Shankar has the bigger appetite.

It wasn't always so. I remember when Shankar was too weak to suck. It was a cycle that started from his first hour. Weakness kept him from sucking, which made him weaker, which kept him from sucking. When his arm worked loose from the swaddling, it hung down. The skin of it slid loosely under the thumb, no baby fat to swell it taut. I could not bear to see the arm dangle like that. I would tuck it up like a broken part and fix the cloth. His palms, his lips, the skin around his lips, and the soles of his feet deepened in colour as he cried. Blue, bluish purple, purple. His colour returned to grey only after his mewl slackened into sleep.

I carried him a lot those first few weeks. The kohl Sonia used to rim his eyes made him look sicker. His brother slept, pink and blissful, after the breast or a bath and rubdown with coconut oil. Shankar was a minute older, but everything gave him a look of age. He had a full head of silken womb hair, while Keshav was baby-bald, just fuzz. What little milk Shankar could get down, he didn't keep down. His oval face hungered from the hour he was born and drew no succour from breath or breast. The shape of his face was another thing that made him look older, especially next to his brother's, a perfect circle broken only by the bulges of his cheeks. I shook my head at the contrast of destinies. By week three, Keshav had put down roots in life and taken. Shankar fitted on Sonia's palm and upturned wrist. She held his sleep like a beggar showing the empty bowl.

My marriage to Sonia had contaminated me, in the opinion of my Brahmin family. So my children by that marriage were likewise impure. Because Sonia had no kin of her own, no one had been present for the birth. My mother had not come, or had been forbidden to come.

I still believed they would all soften, my father included. I half expected, whenever I answered the door, to see them as they had been before, before my contamination. After all, hadn't my father incurred contamination, too, when young, by sailing overseas to the Royal College to study? And by seeing, in his office, patients of every caste and no caste at all, cupping their cracked heels to test the sprain, or kneading their abdomens to find the culprit organ? His choices had been controversial in his day, for the son of a Brahmin family as high and orthodox as his. My grandfather forgave him only because he was second-born. The elder son had memorized the slokas and become a pandit like his forefathers; everything was not lost. A pandit and a ceremony purified my father when he came back. At the train station—this train station—he arrived all those years ago, shoulders sloping asymmetrically, a light bag on the left, on the right a new trunk, filled entirely, it turned out, not with gifts from England but with textbooks. He wore English trousers beside the Vedic fire. Still, certain ideas of blood and caste had never left him. They were objective realities to him, like the height or weight of a person. I know because that is how I thought of it, too, until Sonia.

No quantity of rice or Sanskrit could exculpate me. My betrayal was total, and my contamination was total, my sons' as well. What my family would have thought a divine blessing in other circumstances—twin sons, like Shri Rama himself—now struck them as animal fertility, slum fertility. What caste but the lowest, they reasoned, would have originated my orphan wife? The churches thrived off the people Gandhi was calling 'harijans'. Untouchables: everyone knew what they did to girl children they didn't want—killed them, abandoned them, or sold them to the Christians, who were always in the market for souls.

My elder sister Damyanti visited us once that first hectic month, a shawl over her head and her bag tucked protectively under her arm. It must not have been easy for her to sneak out to us. We had moved to a poorer—that is, Muslim—part of town. The neighbourhood's very name, Nizam Chowk, had a harsh, foreign, faraway sound in our house. It could have been on the other side of a border. Yet she arrived to name my boys. For weeks, Damyanti had tasted names like the sweets a caterer lays out to court the bride's parents. When she learned they were twins, the rules changed, and she tested rhyming names, alliterative names. The meanings, too, were important to her. She could not bear the frivolous Leena-Meena of her best friend's twins. So she settled on naming my boys after Shiva and Vishnu, the destroyer and the sustainer: Shankar and Keshav.

The boys were napping when she arrived at our door, shook off her sandals, and started crying softly. I peeled back the blankets to show her. The showing didn't last long enough, with the swaddling and the caps, for her to see the difference.

She couldn't carry out a full naming ceremony with guests and a pandit, but she did take out a tin that had a single piece of my mother's gajjar mithai. Sonia hovered in the kitchen, and my sister didn't call her over. Eventually Sonia did come out with a tray and a glass of water, but Damyanti declined it. When Sonia was back in the kitchen, my sister looked at me and whispered, 'But I am thirsty, Roshan bhaiyya.' I knew what she meant. I went into the kitchen and, without looking at Sonia, ladled a glass with my own Brahmin hands and brought it to Damyanti. I stood halfway between the two women, Sonia's retiring shadow and Damyanti with her nose turned up, pouring the water into her mouth without letting her lips touch the rim. Between my own two lives. All this she did in my home, to my wife, with a perfect sense of justification—but when she told me the names she had chosen for my sons, I bit the sweet she held out to me and thanked her. Sonia, too, accepted them. This was how newborns were properly named, and I was grateful my twins' names originated where they should have, with the father's sister. It was as though she had salvaged something of their birthright and delivered it.

Keshav started crying and woke Shankar, who had cried longer and so fallen asleep later. Damyanti asked to hold them. She wanted to hold them at the same time. When she had them both in her arms, the first thing she said was, concernedly, looking down at Shankar, 'Isn't she *feeding* this one?'

Sonia sobbed, just once, from inside the kitchen. It did feel, in those early days, like her own failure. She had no one to tell her otherwise, not even me. I won't pretend to some kind of enlightenment back then. I never really understood how she felt—having become a mother without any example of motherhood to refer to, or any older woman's counsel. I expected the know-how to come physiologically, with the milk to the breasts.

So when I took Shankar away from Damyanti, I did it to defend him, not Sonia. To own my firstborn son—not my wife—in proud, defiant love. Of Sonia I was still, in some deep part of myself, ashamed. But Shankar, I sensed, was the victim of some higher malice, and this malice was enough, it was all a creature could bear. I would protect him against every human addition to that malice because I had declared the suffering he was born to suffering enough. So I took him away and held him close, as though my sister had wounded him. Sonia, emboldened, took Keshav back. The boys were screaming now, our agitation contagious. Damyanti gathered her shawl about her, shut the empty tin and put it in her bag, and left. Her sandals clacked down the stairs and vanished over the dust.

Between my two boys, I could have guessed Shankar would get the broken ribs, the worse injury decided by a matter of inches. This is one more piece of bad luck for him I will never understand, no matter how much I read about karma.

It was all I could do, when he was a newborn, to throw my arm out in time and block the curtain rod that fell, without provocation, across his cradle. Later, when he started walking, the house had every corner and edge out for him like knives. I knew the difference because his brother had started walking two months before. I remember Shankar walking into a ball and chasing it, laughing every time it skipped away from him. A scorpion darted from behind our framed portrait of Bala Krishna, and I had to scoop Shankar off the ground.

Even after my sickness started, I was always on the lookout. His face had a strangely grown-up, serious, almost worried look. He sensed the same malice in the cosmos that I did. But when he laughed, I saw his mother's eyes in my own face, eyes that narrowed and curved into darkly shining arches, and I knew the deal I had made with the Gods was being honoured.

The razor drops from Masud's hand. He has forgotten his half-mask of shaving cream and overnight stubble. He looks down. His foot is bleeding, the cut straight, oblique, shallow. The razor is close by his foot, in the dust. He lifts his foot and puts it down, not knowing what to do. A weak gesture, as if to show someone the calamity. The flames have used treetops as a bridge on to his terrace. No one is there to see it with him. The other houses are empty; they had means, and they left in time.

Standing beside him, I stare at the smoke over his house. Shapes of smoke curl, hold, and release: a woman is underwater, her hair, undone, floating vertically; a man's face turns aside and splits down the middle; two children embrace until parted by a wind. Blacker, thicker smoke rises and curls into itself. Everything is prefigured. Masud sees smoke. I see what I have foreseen.

It's not that Masud doesn't know what has happened to the Punjab. He owns a radio—not a good one, but the radio would have to break completely before it occurred to him to replace it. Even if he didn't, there was no way not to hear, if nothing else then at the clinic. The BBC has been discussing the issue for some time. He knew this great event was coming, but he understood the new border only in the abstract, an understanding as simple as a mapmaker's or an Englishman's. A line demarcating jurisdictions, not identities. He cannot hear the radio's static for what it is—the border's cupful of acid, flung hissing into the soil.

Congress and the Muslim League had pounded their tables and made their speeches. Why should it alter his routine? His day has been unalterable for years now. His life takes place almost entirely inside the clinic. He gets in at nine in the morning and stays twelve, sometimes fourteen hours, even though he could leave earlier. His stammer and intense shyness keep him from easily navigating any interaction more complicated than question, examine, advise. The rare times he goes out to buy toothpaste or tea, he points with his middle finger, furrows his brow, nods or shakes his head in great, exaggerated rolls and jerks. He is pious, on the surface of it, but his prayers are merely one component of a larger, daily routine. The mind stays quite blank.

Masud is an innocent. He has seen these people, Sikh, Muslim, Hindu, only as parents worried about their suffering children. Vulnerability, compassion, devastation. They have waited to see him shoulder to shoulder, drawn to his name from nearby villages. The children from the villages are always far gone before they get to him, their abscesses the size of his fist, diphtheria swelling their necks like a sounding toad's. He has always seen the parents mixed democratically along the overcrowded clinic corridors, backs chalked with whitewash where they sat leaning against the walls, stroking the meek, sleepless heads in their laps.

A turn of his head, then his whole body, shows him the extent of what has happened overnight. His block is not the only one burning. The city is bleeding smoke into the sky. It's taken the smell of smoke to prove to him he isn't Ibrahim Masud to anyone but himself now. His profession, too, means nothing. *Muslim*: that's suddenly the defining thing about him. The only detail, everything around it effaced. When did this happen? The official line is that he can stay if he wants or leave for Pakistan. His choice—stay here in India or shift west. Just over there. Like crossing the aisle on a bus.

Masud hurries inside, skipping once from the pain in his foot. The smoke stings his eyes. His cough sounds at different points in the haze. Trousers, shirt, money, glasses, shoes. These are to be expected. But he also takes his black doctor's bag. As though he could let the house burn but must not be late to work. He will go to the clinic because the clinic is the only place he feels safe. It feels protected from further suffering because of the suffering already there. Violence would not trespass on the dominion of illness.

His bicycle seat and pedals fit themselves as always to his body, and he cycles, his speed no different than on any other day, down his usual route. The only difference is that no one is out, and broken glass and smoking trash heaps litter the street. His pulse has just gone calm, given this pacifier of familiarity, when he rounds a corner to find vultures. At least three dozen of them crowd the street and rooftops. At regular intervals down the street, they pose atop the street lamps the British put up fifteen years earlier. Some groom themselves, others meditate. The death here is old. This convocation is thick as seagulls along a shore.

A dog trots past and weaves among the bodies as though to show him a way through. One shoe on the ground, one on a pedal, Masud looks back, around the corner, wondering about the smoking heaps he has passed. He gets off and walks the bicycle.

His progress is slow up a crooked runnel of limbs and wings. The chain clicks. He keeps his eyes on the passage between the bodies, not the bodies themselves. The vultures poke, shuffle to a more suitable angle, and poke again. He thumbs his bell. They make way, a fluster of wings, a reluctant hop. He thumbs the bell twice more, turning the handlebars, stepping carefully. The road was never so long. It takes whole minutes of walking this way before he can get back on and pedal. He stands on the pedals because everything feels uphill now. At last, he stops before his clinic. He gets off and holds the seat a while, looking. Finally his hand slides to his side, and the bicycle tips away from him. He lets it fall. The rear wheel turns slowly in the air.

This is the clinic where, years earlier, we had travelled with the boys. Dr Ibrahim Masud had a reputation that had travelled as far east as Delhi and as far west as our own city. Sonia's midwife, Haleema bibi, who had over several visits fallen into the role of grandmother and counsellor, spoke of his knowledge with the same voice such women use when speaking of their superstitions. He alone, she declared, running her ancient hand over Shankar's head, he alone would *know*.

I had heard of him from my own father, years ago. In his final year in London, my father had been introduced to this young Punjabi who was just starting his studies. Masud was, at that time, only seventeen. My father had expected to take him for a fitting at the nearest tailor's and help him find Indian food; to warn him which instructors would be hostile to him, which ones indifferent; to speak their warm home language after a long day of anatomy Latin.

Yet Ibrahim needed no companionship and felt, it seemed, no homesickness at all. He had got the year's textbooks while still in India and was able to recite them rocking back and forth, as religious students did the Qur'an. A recording, impossible to converse with. The chapter on chronic pulmonary phthisis from Eustace Smith's *On the Wasting Diseases of Infants and Children* tumbled out fluently. Ibrahim's own name, though, came out 'Ib ib ibbbbb', like uncontrollable hiccups.

Years later, my father came across Masud's study of plague deaths in the Amritsar and Kasur districts, published in the *Indian Medical Archives*. It was the writing my father would have expected of him: meticulous accounting, like a census-taker's, but no interpretation, no commentary. Data without an idea, more tables than words.

I bring it before my vanished eyes and read. This is how Masud's mind worked. Something verbal, perceptual, emotional was missing. For all that, his mind contained his field. The two best-known paediatricians in Lahore shook their heads over Shankar and pointed us east to Masud.

The boys slept well on the train. Our arms and the compartment embedded rocking motion inside rocking motion. We took the same Amritsar-bound train, at the same hour, that Sonia and the boys would try to take years later. They would be separated from their mother only four compartments over.

At one point, the boys woke and started crying. It wasn't that one woke up the other. Rather both boys threw out their arms as if dropped from a height and couldn't be consoled for some minutes. Finally the breast calmed Keshav, who drank his fill and drowsed with his mouth in place. Sonia and I traded babies so she could try the same with Shankar, who sucked only a few seconds, burrowed towards her, and fell asleep. I wonder if the moment they woke was the moment we crossed the as yet undrawn border between Pakistan and India. Did they sense something seismic there, a future rift in the earth, the way animals get skittish before a coming earthquake? Did they sense the fault line?

I can still picture Masud warming the cup of his stethoscope in his hand as he stroked my son's head. The doctor had trouble speaking, it was true, but only to adults. Around the children, his stammer eased. Sentences, short ones, came out whole, two sometimes in succession. And so the child became an intermediary through whom he could communicate to the parents, even if the child were Shankar's age. He spoke facing Shankar, addressed his questions as if directly to the infant in my arms, and I answered—how often his skin went blue, whether he took small feedings frequently or none at all, whether his twin had any such troubles. When Masud brought up the stethoscope earpieces, I noticed the gentle fringe of hairs along his ears. He listened using the bell and the flat to

Shankar's chest and back. My boy propped in my lap, with the blankets and clothes undone, I realized anew how tiny he was. Even the child-sized stethoscope, its bell no bigger than a coin, seemed large against his ribs. Sonia must have seen him bare like this every day when soaping, rinsing, drying him, a droplet of oil in the palm enough to rub him down. I closed my eyes and felt relieved, when his examiner sat back, to wrap his starvation-thin body.

'Your pappa is a doctor, hm?' Masud said.

I nodded.

He looked at Sonia and raised a finger to tell her to wait there with Keshav. Then he led me, Shankar in my arms, into his personal office, and said in English, pointing at his heart, 'Blue disease.' He tilted books down from a wall of them, books so thick the highest ones had to be caught on the other palm.

Diagrams of the heart and great vessels showed the red aorta curving through the chest and sprouting branches, and the pulmonary artery, painted blue, splitting in half. He angled his fist against his chest and began to explain, the fingers of one hand splaying, the fist opening and closing. His speech became fluent as he quoted the texts laid out before me. I nodded, but I was only pretending to understand, the way I used to as a boy beside my mathematics tutor—so much passion, so much desire to communicate, that I felt ashamed it should be wasted. I wanted to reward the trouble taken over me.

I understand it now, of course. I can see inside Shankar's chest, past the three intensely painful broken ribs. I see the narrowed corridor through which his blood must pass on the way to his lungs, and the tiny new vessels his heart has desperately let down, like banyan shoots, to get the blood where it has to go. I lay open the book of his chest.

Back then, in spite of my own medical training, I understood only that something deep and unreachable in my son was flawed. I am not sure if Masud had finished speaking when I asked, 'Is he going to live?'

Masud did what he did whenever the answer was no. He showed the backs of his hands, as if in namaaz, and looked at the sky. In that moment, when he referred me to heaven because there was no hope on earth, the bargain was made. In my heart, without the formality of prayer or the striking of a temple bell, I offered all I had. What was surrendered would be collected, and what was granted would be distributed, very slowly, over the next year. But at that moment, imperceptibly, my son began to thrive, and I let in my sickness unto death.

Masud's hands are now crossed over his mouth. Broken glassware, forceps, two steel basins and several boiled-sterile scalpels clutter the stone walk. They have been thrown from the room upstairs where he lances abscesses and extracts splinters. He limps inside, his left shoe soggy with blood from the razor cut. It doesn't occur to him to check if the people who did this have left or not. On his way upstairs, he passes a sink and mirror and sees shreds of shaving cream still bearding one cheek. An intense flush goes over his face and neck. The world has gone to havoc, but his person must not surrender to it. The taps still work. Carefully, in the ruins of his clinic, he tries to finish his interrupted shave. A scalpel off the floor serves as razor, not a kind edge to use. Two fat drops of blood spot the sink. He stops and splashes off the shaving cream. So his face remains divided, one side clean-shaven, shadow on the other.

Upstairs, a tall steel cabinet's linens and towels have been scooped on to the floor and kicked about—no other quick way to vandalize towels. A crowbar threads the handles, paint scraped bright from the rough force-through. Inside that cabinet, a muffled voice.

'33 Firoza Bagh,' it sobs. '33 Firoza Bagh, just past the Ganesh temple . . . please let me out . . .'

The address is Masud's own. He recognizes, after a moment, the voice of Gul Singh, his errand-runner and gatekeeper. He draws out the crowbar. Gul Singh has been stuffed into the bottom shelf, half his size; his body, once it writhes on to the floor, seems to expand. 'I'll tell you, my brothers, I'll tell you where . . .' His face turns up to see Masud through eyes nearly swollen shut. He stops speaking and hangs his head.

Masud kneels. Gul Singh raises his head.

'I didn't tell them, doctor sahib. I swear.'

He is telling the truth. The proof colours his cheek and eyes black-purple. Locked in the cabinet, he grew scared they would set fire to the clinic—so he gave up the address, but after they left. He is ashamed nonetheless, and Masud cannot bring him to his feet.

'You have to go,' moans Gul Singh. 'This city isn't safe for you.'

Masud gestures at the room. 'This? This?'

Gul Singh explains how it is the same all over the city, every Muslim shopfront a blown-in cavity of ash, flanked by intact Hindu or Sikh shops. Small photographs of Sikh women mutilated in Rawalpindi pass from hand to hand. Their naked backs or foreheads have been scrawled upon like the walls of a demolished gurdwara: *Aslam Khan ki biwi*. 'Wife' of Aslam Khan. The group that came through looking for the rich Mussulmaan doctor spared Gul Singh because of his kes and kara, but loyal silence earned him fists to the face. He knew two of the boys—Sukhdev Kang's sons, though they didn't admit to knowing him. They are pious sons of a pious father, and, for all his personal loyalty to Dr Masud, there is a part of Gul Singh, too, that believes what is happening is necessary. Some killing must be done. It is a form of communication, the only kind that can cross the partitions between this country and its neighbour, between this world and the next. Their enemies must hear the deaths, and know fear; their dead must hear the deaths, and know rest. This Mussulmaan, this one, is a good man, thinks Gul Singh—this *one*. With his arms around the doctor sahib's bony knees, he begs him to leave the city.

Outside, Masud's bicycle is being tilted upright by three children. One gets on the ledge behind the pedaller, but the smallest child needs to sit in the basket. Masud's black doctor's bag, after being shaken out curiously, is tossed on the road. The children do not think of this as stealing. They figure whoever fell off the bicycle has long since been dragged away.

The city isn't safe for any Mussulmaan, Gul Singh is pleading, much less a rich doctor. Hadn't they come this morning especially for him? He must leave—but not on the trains. Gul has been hearing about it since last night, there are plans for the westbound trains. Gifts to Pakistan.

Masud bites his lip, looks around, and nods. Part of him wants to start putting everything back where it was, sweep up the glass, fold the towels, boil the scalpels clean. A broken window cuts his gaze as his gaze goes through it. It shows him the once-familiar street changed, the city itself changed, the country. He must go. He has nowhere to go. He must go.

• Two •

Departures

Keshav locks his ankles and bare palms around the platform's corner pillar. He looks up. A sparrow has stashed straw under the awning. It sweeps in from nothingness, hops twice, comments, hops again. It watches the mayhem of adults below, and, tilting its bird neck, the scoot and effort of this child. Hand over hand, then the knees come up. He slides back down. The silk of his shirt snags the eczematous paint. His palms smell sour. Shankar gets his shoulder under his brother's rear and stands, pushing him higher. He lets go of his own snapped ribs so he can hold his brother in place with both hands.

'Do you see her?'

'I'm looking, bhaiyya.'

'Go higher, so she can see you.'

Sweat stings a line down Keshav's scraped cheek, dividing blood and blood. He nods and gets nowhere. His wrists cord, his tiny arms shake as if in frustration. I could have lifted him on to my shoulders, secured his knees and let him see over everybody. They were just getting old enough for me to do that when I fell ill.

Keshav is barely above the level of the waves. He is looking among them for a single wave. The waters themselves are starting to roil. The people outside the station have crushed on to the platform. A man scuffles on to the empty tracks, arms out. He trips on the rails, falls, leaps to his feet. Throwing his arm forwards, he shouts something, then runs towards the platform and climbs back into the crowd. Immediately the crowd starts stirring violently there; the first fight of several has begun.

The stationmaster, his back against his office door, blows a whistle several times, like a police officer. Sensing the riot coming, and fearful now that he has drawn attention to himself, he lets the whistle drop on to the dome of his belly and slides into his office. Keshav can see him through the window as he drags his desk and file cabinets to block the door. The shutters slam shut, but the weather-warped wood no longer fits as it was first planed. Four rough yanks force them flush before the iron hooks align with their hook holes.

Keshav squints over the crowd like a lookout in a crow's nest. The ocean, though made of people, is lonely.

Looking down the platform for his mother, Keshav is facing north; Masud, in his clinic, looking through the broken window, north as well. My attention, too, turns north, over the Jhelum and Chenab. These aren't the only rivers I pass. There are rivers of people as well. The first kafila gives me pause. I hover and take in the wooden carts, the shrunken oxen, occasional human bodies ditched on the side like abandoned vehicles—the soul recognizing a surer, instantaneous escape, and taking it.

I could bring my face close enough to every face here that if I breathed they would feel it, all of them at once, as a breeze.

Maybe some of the thousands of dead are doing this even now, just before they leave for good—blowing once on every forehead, and vanishing.

The wind would make a good gift, as this season is the hottest in decades. Not that I feel temperatures any more. I infer the heat from the shirts, soaked transparent and later stained yellow, of farmers used to heat but not to heat like this. That and how often I see them wipe their sleeves across their foreheads. Punjab is a dry pan left on the flame. The first drops of rain, if they come, may well pop and hiss.

It is a temptation, I admit, to spread my attention up and down each kafila I overfly. The temptation I feel is not as intense, though, as the one I felt five years ago, bedbound, under my shawls. The living think of that moment as a slackening, the limbs going weak, a sleep that is to sleep what sleep is to waking. To my surprise, the moment came as a surge of energy. I felt power-ful enough to divide infinitely, which is what most people do, of course. Afterwards, there's no gathering them. So I am careful to hold myself together. I keep my thumb over the nozzle of that energy. I slip it aside to soar north and quickly slide it back again. I arrive.

Only God's houses are brick in this village. A yellow flag marks the gurdwara, a cluster of shoes and sandals the mosque. The other houses, the colour of earth, slope out of the earth. Electricity has reached here—a cord lies black against a wall and vanishes through a window as small as a ship's porthole.

She is one of five children. Four daughters and a precious son. The son is youngest. Her parents had a child every two years until they had a son. After the son, they could stop, the name preserved and the blood safe. I am here to see her because I have traced her from her future back to this spot.

In these three crowded rooms, her father's elder brother and his two grown sons have taken refuge. Where their wives are, they do not say. Squatting, elbows on their knees, they spread on the earthen floor stories like blood-soaked rags. The mother and daughters must crowd into the bedroom; they are locked there, along with the boy, who is only six and not yet old enough to want to be with the men. He is happier here, covering his eyes with his mother's dupatta, ignoring the nervous murmurs of his sisters.

She is in that room, with the others. She maintains the reserve befitting the eldest daughter. She is barely fifteen. Simran. How solemn she looks, as if she senses everything to come. Her little brother, Jasbir, tires of his mother's dupatta and rests his head in her lap. Simran rubs his velvety ear between her thumb and forefinger, the way he likes. I watch her fingers, rhythmic, gentle, and strangely delicate for one who does so much washing, milking, husking. Her movements remind me of the regular, meditative way a mala circulates through holy fingers. One of her younger sisters sneaks over to the door to try to listen. Simran glances at her mother, who clicks her tongue and gestures the girl back. Her mother is just as curious, and so is Simran, about what the men are saying, but still she calls her back. It's not that she wants her children to stay calm, or to let her children stay children this half-hour longer. Rather fear, almost superstitious, makes her keep her children close to her. Not hearing their taya's stories, she feels, will protect them. To hear the horror will bring it into being.

The men whisper too softly to be heard anyway, even in that small house. Their women, they are saying—without tears, without guilt—are *safe*. A pistol lies in one of the grown son's palms. It is wrapped in bright purple cloth. He drops the ends of the cloth and holds the gun flat on his palm. The women have been smuggled to a place where they cannot be touched. Two nights ago, every door in the village had started shaking, as though a train were coming through full speed. There hadn't been much time. There is not much time now. Does he have morphine in the house? Not to keep them quiet, his women are strong, just as theirs were, and they would not try to run away.

Simran's father puts his hands over his eyes and shakes his head. I do not know what he does not want to see: the sight of his brother telling him what must be done, or the vision of him doing it. Or the vision of what will happen to his wife and children if he doesn't. Of the three, this last is the one he cannot bear.

The Mussulmaans, says his brother, came with scythes the shape of the crescent on their new flag, shovels stolen off farms on the way in, butcher knives until then used only for halal killing. Clubs with nails sticking out of them, shovels edged with dried blood. Lathis of varying lengths and woods. Hammers, both the curved end and the flat. One even swung an Englishman's walking stick.

'And Jasbir?'

'He'll slow us down.'

'You never know when we'll have to run, chacha. What will you do? Carry him?'

'There are Mussulmaans who would love to have a boy. Save him.'

'How can I do this?'

'How we did it. Harpreet will help.'

'He did the work back home.'

'After this, I am joining up. We have our own armies, across the border. I will go to Amritsar, pray there for strength, and join.'

'What do we do first?'

'Do you have any morphine?'

'Some. For her tooth, last year.' Simran's father has never, except after making love, said his wife's name, not directly, not in reference to her. 'There's not much left of it.'

'Is it a powder?'

'No.' He raises thumb and forefinger. 'A bottle. A little bottle.'

'That's better.'

'Will it be enough?'

Harpreet nods. 'They are small girls.'

Harpreet's younger brother, who has been holding the pistol, sets it before his knees and brings the folds across it reverently, as though covering the Granth. More whispers.

I go back to Simran, still rubbing her brother's ear. It makes him drowsy. So I am with her when the latch grates across. It chills her to discover that the door was secured from without. The door opens. Her father stands in the doorway, gazing at this group huddled at the other end of the room. His brother, he realizes, is right. It must be done; it is the only way to protect them. If annihilation were all, then they might as well risk flight. But the women and the boy risked something worse. To live in their shacks: his girls their wives, daily servitude, nightly violence, in a few years not even remembering their true nature. Coming to smell as they smell, eat as they eat. Bearing Muslim sons who would grow up never knowing their grandfather was a Sikh steely as his kangan and proud. Conversion. To bow to their holy city, kiss their book, recite their prayers. Die now and they would die Sikhs, intact, pure in the eyes of the ten Gurus. Dying a Sikh, for being a Sikh: this must be the women's glory. For the men, there would be valour in the streets yet, and blood on the kirpan. But neither he nor his, he decides, will live as anything else. Better annihilation than long life giving some slum Mussulmaan pleasure and service and sons. So when her mother whispers, 'What did they say?', his voice is calm.

'Heat us up some milk.'

Her mother visibly relaxes, this domestic request somehow proof that the threat has either passed, or never was. 'What do you want in it?'

'Cardamom. And make enough for all of us.'

'Should we come out?'

'Not yet.'

'Is it true? Are the mobs close?'

Her father looks first over his shoulder, then back at his daughters. The swell of pride and defiance, just moments earlier, has petered out. His hands go over his chest and start kneading each other. 'The milk,' he says.

Jasbir sits up. 'Let them come. They'll see what we Sikh boys can do.'

Her mother says, 'Simran, go.'

Simran rises and hurries past her father. Her taya and her cousin do not look at her. One looks at the ground, the other at a small dark blue bottle in his hand. Harpreet doesn't look at her, either, but his eyes are closed. He is sitting cross-legged on the floor, something wrapped in purple cloth in front of him, not a book. His lips move in a prayer to which he gives no voice.

Thirty-six miles east of the station, the train my boys have jumped from will hiss to a stop. Ravine to one side, empty farm to the other. A solitary boy, not more than fourteen, fuzz across his top lip, green-eyed, is going to lower the colourful flag he has been waving. It is a stick with a girl's choli nailed to it. Little sewn-in hexagons of mirror, bright pink and orange paisley, the kind of thing young village girls wear. He will step off the tracks, drop the stick with the choli, and pick up an axe. The train will be a half-hour from any station, east or west. Twenty minutes from the border.

This signal and this spot were arranged at the station in Pakistan, while Sonia and my boys were still in the crowd. Six bearded men had boarded the front car. They had no weapons. They had come to talk.

The driver, a Hindu named Chandan Singh, will see the

signal and pray. He will tug his earlobes and crank the lever to scrape this train to a halt. In his defence, he had refused to do it for money, or at least for the money they offered. They had to say his address to him and tell him how many children he had and how old. After that, they refused him any money at all. As if by requiring the threat, he had lost the privilege of being bought fairly. Right now, as his train rushes towards the far convergence of rails, and Keshav is shouting the word *Ma* over six hundred heads, Chandan regrets that he did not agree right away. At least there would have been money. The lost opportunity makes him flush under his beard. That will change, of course, when he is actually confronted with the killing. Or rather with the sounds of the killing—he will face forwards the whole time, his hands still on the levers, focused on the track ahead. He will not see the men stride out of the ravine bearing axes and farm tools like itinerant workers. Or how unhurried they are. Well after dark, a stick will rap the side of his car, the way bus passengers tap the side of the bus to say they have got off. Chandan will shift the levers, this one forwards, this one back, and he will coast his cargo across the border, never speeding beyond the lightest, softest rock and click.

It will be midnight by the time the train makes it into the station, every compartment closed and locked, door and window. At Amritsar, the crowd on the platform will sense something wrong about the train well before it stops. People will start pressing back from the tracks while the train is still a dot of light no bigger than a star. The platform will stay quiet as the train inches into place. The absence of anyone on the roof, maybe, or the emptiness of the windows. The stationmaster will part the crowd and throw wide a compartment door. The first gush will reach his feet. He will skip back and leave his sandals in place, soaked, the bottom step still dripping.

A clamour of pots pulls my attention back in time to the present. Simran has been clumsy, and she is never clumsy. Her father walks over to check. Kerosene odour, milk placid in the pot, the flame adjusted to a blue corona. The cups have been drying on a rack. Still wet. One end of her dupatta lies on her palm, the other covers her small fist. She turns each cup twice around her fist and sets it down. Most of the drops are on the outside. Her father circles back.

'Six,' he says, intervening before she dries any for the men. Each cup is a death, in his mind, and he does not want any more prepared.

She lines up five cups beside the stove.

'One more.'

She looks up. 'I'm not thirsty.'

'You'll *drink*.'

This is enough, the words, and the agitation that has overtaken his hands and feet. Her father paces, he makes and unmakes a fist with his left hand, checking the flame and the milk. The right hand he holds in a fist over his heart, as if taking a vow to protect something. Simran wonders at that. She doesn't know that the hand has the vial in it. Her younger cousin had gone out and now comes back through the door. He stops when he sees her. Harpreet breaks his meditation. The men drift to the door and get the news. Simran's father breaks away abruptly and points at Simran.

'Pour it out and go back in the room.' She doesn't move quickly enough. 'Pour it *out!*'

The lukewarm milk splashes over the sides of the cups. His jitter is close to panic now and contagious. Two of the cups, silver, have tiny letters engraved just under the rims. They are name-day cups, given to honour a new child, full name and birth date. Once-bright cups, saved in a chest for some years, and finally, for want of money to buy new ones, fallen into daily circulation. The letters are uneven, done by an untrained silversmith's hand that used the point like a pen. Simran sees her own cup. She has seen it so often, in the after-dinner pile and in her siblings' hands, she has ceased to think of it as hers. By the time it came out of the chest, she had been too old to claim it or demand it. But now, for the first time in years, she notices her name, and she thinks, just for a moment, of her birth. Of herself as a newborn in this very house, her father's beard black and her mother just two years older than Simran is now.

'Leave them there.'

She rises off her knees, her legs seemingly unaware of her weight, a movement whole and graceful. She stands as tall as her father. Then she is back in the room, her mother and sisters and brother sitting. She keeps standing after the door closes and the latch grates into place again.

'Milk? This early in the morning?' Her mother searches Simran's profile. 'And a morning like this?'

'It's for us.'

Her mother says nothing more. Simran steps back until she touches the wall and slides to the ground.

Keshav's arms ease around the pillar, and Shankar steps away as his brother lowers himself.

'I can't see her.'

Shankar looks in the direction the train disappeared. I can see him wondering if they have made a mistake. He turns back to the crowd. Surges and calms seem to overtake it independently of any event on the tracks or platform. Keshav shouts for their mother, and Shankar joins him, call and call and no answer, their search party stalled at the edge of this Dandaka forest of legs. Shankar leaves off before Keshav, who redoubles his effort, hands to either side of his mouth. Their voices are small. No one hears, not even the people immediately in front of them. Some are arguing, some are covering their mouths, some are shaking their heads. I see Shankar has an idea.

'Keshav!'

'*Ma!*'

He tugs his brother's blood-wet sleeve. 'Keshav. Let's go down there. She'll see us.'

They hold hands and scoot off the platform at the spot where Shankar had just fallen. Shankar is excited enough by his idea that he forgets, for a while, about his chest. I focus on those hands, small hand around an even smaller one. I wish I could make a chain of three and lead them out of this. They keep walking until they are on the tracks, facing the centre of the platform. They show themselves. Shankar's idea is to set his brother and himself apart, make them visible, give their mother the best chance of finding them. Or if she asks around whether anyone had seen two boys, this old, wearing this, there is a good chance someone will nod and point to the tracks. The problem is that no one is looking. I scan their minds. Not one spike of pity. Glances brush the tracks but don't snag. Such beautiful little twins, bloodied, in torn and dusty silk, but they are background. Keshav gets the balls of his feet on to a rail and tiptoes, all the height he can get, and starts up his shouting, as unheard as he is unseen. Boy shoulders thrown back, chin in the air, *Ma!* His eyes clench shut with each shout because he has lost hope in his eyes finding her. All his hope is in his voice. Shankar stares down the tracks and wonders, again, if she was on the train all along. Did they *see* her get off the train? Hadn't she got on the steps before she let them pull themselves aboard? The panic of separation gives way to a falling feeling, dizziness, a flush up the sides of his face. They are alone.

Gul Singh stares down the empty street. He tugs his beard.

Masud is collecting the contents of his doctor's bag. The bag itself he found upside down. He rushed to it as to a fallen child. It is leather, purchased years ago in London. He slaps the surface of scuff. 'How will you get there without your cycle, doctor sahib?' Masud doesn't answer. On both knees, he reaches for each instrument, inspects it, and cleans it as best he can before placing it in the bag kept open at his side. A probe and lancet slide pale dust stripes on his trouser leg. A paediatric blood pressure cuff, and the soft bulb to inflate it. Two clamps, one with long curved prongs and one with short straight ones. A 1944 pharmacopoeia, pages swollen crackly from two monsoons ago when he left it by an open window. His implements all go back in the bag, and they will all come with him on his journey. They will provide for him and help him provide. The stethoscope is the same one that listened to Shankar's chest. It picked up the muted dub and faint, steady whoosh that first told Masud what was wrong. Once he told me what to listen for, I couldn't ignore it. Sometimes, on quiet nights, I would seal my ear to Shankar's chest and listen for myself. *So close*, I would think. *Just an inch in, but unreachable.*

His bag assembled and clicked shut, Masud stands. Gul Singh has moved, unaware of himself, off the street and inside the broken gate of the clinic. Masud can read the worry even from his profile, how his gaze follows his imagination down the street. Masud tries to say something, but the words catch. Startled into the present, Gul Singh looks to him, but Masud puts his hand palm out and rolls his head, eyes closed, in a way that means *stay*.

'No, doctor sahib, you can't go alone. Not as far as the police station. Once you get there, everything will be all right, they will put you in a car and drive you away. The policewallahs know you, they know you can pay.' He grabs the lathi he keeps propped beside his gatekeeper's chair. In spite of the ransacking, it is still upright, overlooked, neither snapped nor stolen. Gul Singh never used it much except to rap the occasional cow from the flowers he had planted just inside the clinic gate. Masud shakes his head again and touches the lathi, which drifts back, tamed, to the wall. Because of his trouble with words, Masud can sense the meaning in the way that lathi gives under his hand. No matter what Gul Singh says next, he wants to be persuaded not to come along. 'You need me to protect you, sahib. Haven't I guarded this gate sixteen years now? I will get you to the police station. It's too many blocks away, sahib.'

Masud points at Gul Singh, then cups his hand on an imaginary head. 'Your children,' he says. 'Go make sure.'

A few more exchanges, Gul Singh refusing, Masud insisting—until finally, relieved, Gul Singh asks, 'You know where the station is, right? Straight.' He points. 'Straight.'

Masud nods and points the same way.

'I will clean everything up, sahib. I will get the glass and the mirrors replaced while you are gone. I will take care of everything. As soon as you return, you will start seeing patients. It will be like before.' He is already outside the gate. Unexpectedly, he joins his palms and lowers his head, the way he has done whenever Masud has handed him his wages. Then he turns and rounds the corner and is gone.

Masud waits a while with his arms down, black bag at his side, rail-thin in the English-style trousers tight against his crane-like stick-legs. A last look at his ruined clinic, then he sets off into the emptiness.

· · ·

In a strange reversal, Simran's father comes in holding the tray. For the first time, he is serving them. It looks odd to Simran, almost laughable, to see him doing this. He sets the tray on the floor and looks at Simran's mother, who nods. She understands what is happening. When she sees that nod, Simran, too, understands. Her sisters follow their mother's lead and reach for cups. Simran takes two, one for her, one for Jasbir. By no coincidence she gets her name-day cup. Jasbir starts drinking right away. Simran holds hers. Her youngest sister makes a face. 'Drink,' her father says. Harpreet checks through the doorway and disappears again, top-heavy shoulders and the stone-hard knot of the turban. 'Drink,' her mother repeats, and she raises her cup a little but aborts and holds it in front of her, lips pursed white, nauseous maybe. She says a prayer and tries again, and this time she drinks it all in hurried gulps. Her throat bobs.

Simran is watching. She is certain now, and her heartbeat announces it, so strong I feel it through the air. In fact I feel it inside myself. It is almost like being alive. Simran puts her mouth to the rim and tilts the cup. My hand shoots out, scared for her. She isn't supposed to drink. I hurry closer and look over her shoulder. The milk laps warmly at her upper lip. She hasn't opened her mouth. Her father is watching them; she is watching him, too, over the cup. When the others bring theirs down, she does hers. He is satisfied.

After the door has shut them in again, the cups are set, empty, on the tray. Simran holds hers close and rises.

'Simran?' The drug has not taken effect yet, and her mother straightens; she has been slumped until now with the passivity of prey. 'What are you doing? Come away from that window right now. You can't let the street see in here. All these girls—those mians will be drawn to us like wolves.'

Simran taps the wooden shutter's hook out of its eyehole and shoves. Smoke smell and furnace heat mix with the room's locked-in sweat smell. Her forehead expects a touch of breeze but gets none. Inside hot equals outside hot. Decorative iron blocks off any escape through the window, and besides, she is too big to fit through it. At best, she might have pushed Jasbir to safety—and to the danger safety meant. With a secretiveness new to her, she tilts herself to obstruct her mother's view, and pours out the milk. A channel darkens the wall.

'Priya,' she hears her mother say behind her, 'sit back down and wait!'

Her youngest sister has hurried over and holds up her almost full cup. 'I wasn't thirsty either, didi,' she whispers.

Simran grabs the cup in one hand and Priya's arm in the other. She flings the drugged milk through the window, unabashed now. The cast-iron work and half-open shutter drip. Her mother leans heavily and makes a grab for Priya, but Simran jerks her aside. The children are speechless, even Jasbir. Simran takes three rushed steps to the door. Her sister shuffles after, her arm extended. Simran's mother shouts in alarm. The door shudders once as Harpreet yanks it close to loosen the slide of the latch from its hole. He doesn't expect her and Priya so close, and the gun is at his side. Simran ducks to Priya's height and charges past Harpreet at waist level.

Her cousin's hip bone clips her collarbone about where Shankar hit his in the fall from the train—but this works to her advantage, as it jolts Harpreet aside. Priya slips through behind her. Screams from inside the room, and screams, too, from Priya, who doesn't understand she is being saved—she holds her hand out to their father when he reaches for her. Simran pulls at Priya and sees her father's hand wrap around the small wrist. She gathers her sister in her arms. The gun goes off. Her sister's body jerks in her arms. Startled, Simran drops her. Her mother is in the doorway, wailing. Harpreet, distracted, looks her way. For a moment, everyone in that small house is still. Simran alone is running—dream-running, her legs never moving fast enough. Her kameez is sweat-dark at the armpits and back, and her dupatta is gone. The heat has made the pulled-taut hair frizz around her face. It catches the sunlight and makes a kind of halo. From one direction, she hears the sound of a drum. Any direction but that. She bolts. Impatient gunshots from inside the house close off her childhood for ever. She runs lightly. The balls of her feet leave hare-tracks up the dry dirt road.

The man beating that drum is named Dera Ismail. The strap makes a diagonal on his back. He is the only one in the crowd who doesn't carry a dagger or a sword. His hands are busy on the sides of his drum, and his face is ecstatic, mouth open, eyes closed. Behind him, blades jab at the sky, and the occasional skip or jig gives things the air of a wedding procession. Which is only right, as Dera has played at hundreds of weddings, in this village and those surrounding it. Hindu and Sikh weddings, too, not just Muslim ones. He has a reputation for playing any drum well, pakhawaj, tabla, dhol—and has amused children, at several of those weddings, by feats of percussion using his fingers to slap the grooves between his knuckles, or two spoons, or a handful of marbles. With the marbles, what he did was closer to juggling. Tap, bounce, bounce, a sweep of his hand, the sharp marble-on-tile notes intercut with tongue clicks and water-drip noises he made with his lips. When the time came, he shrugged on his dhol, ran to the gathering crowd, and whistled the way he did to cue his musicians. They cheered when they saw him. He brought an air of festival and ceremony. He is playing his dhol wholeheartedly now, left arm occasionally throwing itself out with panache. Every other job has been just that, a job, flat-fee work for a hired musician, his face indifferent while the groom's brothers and friends danced splendidly around him. Today he inhabits his music. Face up, smiling now. Eyes closed against the sun as he walks. His lids glow red. He could be playing at his own wedding.

Masud watches the street. He is white-eyed and white-knuckled, low and sniffing like a hare hunted into its hole. Behind him, under him, everything is black. Ash inks his cheeks and fingers, soaks his button-down grey. His fingers curl stiffly through the handles of his bag, which he holds at his chin, off the ashes. The ashes under him are soft, papery, still warm. The jeweller's glass counter has melted and dried again, trapping some earrings. They lie stuck to their backdrop. Necklaces of worked, dark yellow gold have long since been looted. The same goes for cylinders displaying brace-lets. From the sign, which said BRILLIANT JEWELLERS—now on the ground, crumpled as though by half a dozen kicks, the sign treated no better than the owner—there was no way to know a man named Atif Khan owned the store. Individually, none of the men knew this, either; only the many had known, and the many had singled it out.

Masud crouches in his black hole, peeking around what is left of the counter. The street stays empty. A sheet of newspaper coasts into view and pauses. A new wind picks it up, and it is gone in a crinkle. Masud waits. What scared him was the sight of three men, far enough off that he could not see their faces or even judge their ages. They hadn't been holding weapons, not that he could see. But he thought ahead—three of them walking on one side of the street, him on the other, bald head down, quick steps, bag fixed at his side—and he could all too easily imagine them crossing, asking his name, asking where he was going. He scurried inside. His footsteps went mute over matted ash. The burned-out jeweller's felt safe the way a cleft tree feels safe in a lightning storm. The violence had visited already and satisfied itself. Too much was still out there for the violence to circle back. Other shops, other people.

This is the eighteenth minute he has been watching the street. Most of this time, he has been motionless. Small noises make his scalp tug. Any noise—once even the crack of his own knee. His ears flick back. His heartbeats crowd close and spread out again.

A few minutes ago, one hand loosened from the bag and combed the ashes beside him. At first pensively, distracted; and now idly, focusing on the texture. His ring finger pricks on something. A splinter? He brings up his hand and sees a tiny gold earring that studs the pad of his finger. It must have dropped during the night's snatching and stuffing. He forgets the pain for a moment; the sight makes him feel as if a lovely winged insect has chosen to alight on his finger. And sting. Blood domes slowly and drips. He sucks his black finger, unhygienic though he knows this to be. The earring he rolls between his thumb and forefinger, meanwhile, and finally slips into his pocket when he stands.

Outside, the daylight shows him wasted and ash-smeared like an ascetic of some wholly other faith. Round black stains on the seat of his trousers mark where his bony pelvis ground the ash hardest. It is this figure that presents itself at the police station half an hour later. The city, as he walked, changed around him. Sparrows became willing to speak again. The hush and curfew lost its hold as the streets broadened. He felt like he was exiting a plague quarantine. But his nerves did not let up. When the first casual bicycle swooped past him, he flinched aside as if he had been struck, and checked over his shoulder. Nothing. More people, open shopfronts, stalls on the roadside. He marvelled how the violence respected borders, how the unspeakable in one place could be conversation in another. There was no partition, no checkpoint or sign, but he had left, appreciably, the Muslim part of the city. The eyes that met his and skipped down his body had no pity in them. Some eyed him with the disgust of the clean for the soiled. Others were simply curious, trying to locate his wounds, find the blood.

Outside the police chowki, he hears paper ripping. Clock-steady, unrelenting. A fan, its blades edged in dust, turns overhead, so slowly it seems the power has just been cut. The thick heat doesn't stir. Two officers stand by a desk at the far end of the building. The other desks are vacant. Filing cabinets stand with their drawers pulled out to varying depths.

One policewallah is ripping pages from a ledger laid out on the desk. The other is checking his work. Even page to the left pile. Odd page to the right pile. Finally all that is left is a cloth cover. Scissors divide this cleanly, along the gum and coarse, frayed threads of the binding. In the lull, Masud steps forwards. He is not the sort to speak up or approach on his own, so the men start on the next ledger, and he has to stand through four hundred more rips. Occasionally he steps outside and puzzles up at the sleeping building, then returns to observe the ritual going on inside. Shouldn't there be alarm bells? Dozens of uniformed young men, rifles on their shoulders, busily running into the street? Reports being written? The policewallahs are bald, elderly men, their paunches administrative. They move on to the dilemma of a telephone. One holds up the receiver, another turns the base upside down, and they discuss the situation without rancour or aggression. A handkerchief dabs a forehead. A shrug, a nod. They have a toolbox on a chair, and a screwdriver is selected for the dismantling.

Masud makes a noise with his throat. They look up from their task. The task has been started, however, and they finish it. Metal parts, the bell and the arm that strikes it, the dial—the telephone is disassembled and collected into a heap of telephone parts. They begin to haggle over each component. They make trades. At last the phone is evenly distributed, and one of the men approaches Masud.

'Yes?'

The sharp, impatient tone paralyses Masud's tongue. He knows himself; it would be futile to try answering. Out of his bag he produces a calling card. One of two hundred he had printed in England four decades ago, when he graduated. A precious chit, wood-textured, the ink letters raised in a way a fingertip could feel. He hopes the officer will hand it back to him, and he does.

'You are a doctor?'

Masud nods, returning the card to his stack.

'No one needs a doctor here.'

Masud zips the bag's inner pocket and looks up.

'What is your business?'

Masud frowns expressively. He points down the street he has just walked. 'That—that—'

'Yes?'

Masud has never encountered the police before. His eyes go to the pistol at the man's waist, the white undershirt visible between his too-taut buttons, the tobacco-stained teeth. The notion of requesting, from this man—what? A jeep ride to safety in Pakistan? And did Pakistan really mean safety? Whom did he know in this conjured country, Pakistan? Where would he knock? Where would he sleep, and what would he put under his head?

Pakistan. It's no longer a question, after what he saw this morning, of *where*, only where *else*. Masud's mouth is open. He feels a surge at the base of his throat that can't break and gush.

The officer glances at Masud's clothes. English-style, ash-blackened, like some gentleman stove-cleaner.

'Do you want to file a report?'

Masud nods because it is the easiest thing he can do. The officer gestures to him to sit. Only there is no bench where he gestures, no chair, only the unswept floor and the wall for backrest. Masud lowers himself and sits with his bag in his lap. The policewallah joins his colleague, who is lazily inspecting the typewriter, pressing one letter very delicately and tentatively: first the resistance, then the give, the key sinking, the typebar rising to strike.

Lying in my cot, propped on three watermelon-shaped pillows, I, too, had waited once. I remember the room exactly. It was all I saw for a year. I got to know the tiles and the patterns of plaster on the ceiling. When the fevers came, and the room was lit by a single moving candle, I saw faces and figures in the spongework. Evenings, I would watch the bugs fleck the wall. The occasional three-fingered lizard. My fellow motionless ones. They basked, I baked.

Shankar and Keshav made of me, as they grew, a kind of playground. They crawled to me in the mornings, pulled up on my cot, and patted me awake with their little hands. I might open my eyes and see one of them face to face. About the kindest way to be awoken to a day of suffering. When they started walking and could climb on to me—my last two months—I was a landscape. Sonia taught them the parts of my face. Eyes, teeth: they would point and say the word. Bloodshot eyes. The teeth I brushed over a steel bowl, too weak to shift into a seated position, just curling forwards at the neck to spit. They were still learning to give kisses when I departed. Not yet the pursed-lips kind of kiss that makes a deliberate click, but a kiss. She would bring them after their baths. That is one of the last images I have: Keshav on her hip; her, leaning to bring his face close; and then the press of his lips on my silvery stubble.

She did make an effort to shave and bathe me regularly. I was careful to gauge how exhausted she was and offer to skip a day. Many nights she fell asleep beside the twins because they would cry whenever she tried to rise. The spread of bedding stayed on the floor, mussed as it was when they awoke from it. I got to fearing Damyanti might hear I had fallen ill and visit again. I did not want her to see the mess and report Sonia's poor upkeep of the flat to my mother and father. Because I was a third child, by then; before I became bedbound, she had been able to keep up.

My practice had been closed for a year. No money was coming in. Hiring her a helper now would mean less savings for when I was gone. I showed her my accounts, the documentation she would need, and the key to the bank deposit box where I stored my first wife's wedding sets—though Sonia swore she would never sell them. We discussed whether she could go back to the church to teach English. I told her she could repent her marriage to me, even raise the boys as Christians, if that was what it took to get help. Such things were all words anyway, I told her, but greatly gratifying to those people.

I wrote to my father and told him, in formal, typewritten English, that the office was his to sell, as I 'would not be practising there any longer'. I made no mention of why. No reference to how my heart, the very muscle of it infected, had ballooned in my chest. (I could feel the tip of it bumping my chest wall by then, in line with the armpit.) Nothing about the fevers, or the way I got winded lifting even little Shankar. I didn't say anything, either, about how well Shankar was doing. My suffering and my joy were both closed off. I had left that life.

At that point, I had already moved us to our new flat. Probably my father assumed I was setting up a new practice. I did not expect him to send me any money from the sale; I had never formally purchased it from him, and the title was still in his name. He didn't disappoint me. At least he hadn't pursued that punishment earlier, selling the building and telling me after the papers were signed. He could have done that. I guess I should have been more grateful and made mention of that in the letter I typed him. But he had been clear that marrying Sonia was the supreme act of ingratitude—to him personally (considering all he had given me), to the memory of my first wife, to my own ancestors going back thousands of years . . . The coldness of my business letter didn't matter. After a crime like mine, what good were niceties? I had listened to his reproaches and asked him, when he paused to wipe his flushed brow, to forgive me. Me, forty-seven years old. Fresh rage shook him and threw his silver hair forward over his brow. That noble head gone wild—I had never been able to oppose him, not as a boy, not as a man. Even as a man, all I could do was run away.

I took us to that new flat when Sonia learned she was pregnant. So early in our marriage! Too early. I changed her life too drastically. I didn't think of that then, of course; in those first months I was experiencing, for the first time in my life, pure sexual exhilaration. I ordered a break in my morning and afternoon schedules to come home to her. She would be waiting for me with the shutters closed and the fan going. Horns, trucks, the sound of the street below, the long wail of the Frontier Mail as it approached city limits—and a steady, greedy slapping in that small hot room, her dark body under my fair-skinned one. For the last minute or so, I would place my hands over her larger scars, or just close my eyes. In time the scars stopped bothering me. She would observe my labours and sometimes intercept, with a fingertip, the sweat before it dripped off my chin or the tip of my nose. It must have been a little game for her. At fifteen years old, a ward of the church, cared for—at seventeen and a half, pregnant with twins, wife to a Hindu man almost thrice her age.

I had made the decision to move hastily, almost out of irritation. The wives in the houses surrounding mine had all been friends of my first wife. They had, over the past eleven years, rotated cooking my meals—and, knowing me to be fairly wealthy, had proposed candidates of their own for my remarriage. I never made an announcement. They assumed, from Sonia's dark skin, that I had hired a new slum girl to clean the house. The first day, one of them asked me if my 'girl' were interested in coming over afterwards; she wanted to see how well she washed dishes, seeing as Nazneen, her usual girl, had been getting careless. I smiled and gave her the good news. She congratulated me to my face, of course, sweetness of speech and formal invitations. By the next day, everyone was speculating, disapproving, making, I am sure, horrified faces. They could see the scars on her arms. What dirt had I tracked into the neighbourhood?

Everyone knew—even the bricklayers, two Muslims, who were laying a new walkway in Ramchand Parikh's courtyard, two houses down. Ramchand owned a steel foundry and could have lived much more extravagantly than he did. Building a new house had struck the penny-pinching Gujarati in him as far too costly, so he had subjected his current home to a series of renovations, collectively cheaper and quicker. Every day, on my way to work, I passed the week's bricklayers, woodworkers, painters or gardeners—maybe the same ones, maybe different. I never looked closely enough to know. We existed on opposite sides of an invisible partition.

The day after word of my marriage got out, though, the bricklayers paused in their work and both raised a hand. I stopped and wondered what to say. I decided on nothing. I raised my hand in return—what else to do?—and walked on, puzzled. Over the next several days, I got more than just raises of the hand. I got smiles, I got salaams, I got a 'sahib'. I was not used to this, being a Brahmin born and a Brahmin still, though happily tainted—quite removed from these ant-hard men and their tasks in the sun. I knew it had something to do with bringing Sonia into my house. Were they mocking me? One day I passed close to one of the bricklayers. He was standing in a sweat-stained kameez with the sleeves rolled up, and drinking from a steel cup. His beard had caught a few drops of the water. I stopped and spoke to him, asking him what Parikh sahib was having them build. I wanted, perversely I know, to see whether he still respected my caste and wealth, whether this Muslim workman could hold back his smirk when answering me.

He set the cup on the wall and started explaining the latest addition to the house, a marble porch with a new swing (Gujaratis loved their swings). His name was Ghulam Sikri, and he was in charge, he said. His muscular arms moved with his words, showing me how much had been done and how much was left to do. He even went into the price of marble. He spoke more openly than I had ever heard one of his kind speak before. The slurrings and contractions of poor men's talk made it a little hard for me to follow. The others rose immediately from their work and nodded as he spoke. There was something more than respect here; there was warmth. They must have overheard my neighbours talking about my choice of wife and realized I had welcomed, for love, the same contempt they suffered for being born, the contempt that in some measure, as much as their faith, defined them. I was, in their opinion, not like my neighbours. In my own opinion, I confess, I still felt apart, superior. I despised my neighbours for despising Sonia, but I felt no sudden kinship, for that reason, to every low-caste or Muslim day-labourer who stank of lamb and slum.

Over the next weeks, though, I did warm to them. They told me their names, they told me the names of their villages. While I was away at work, they spoke to Sonia and redid our bathroom floor in what I am certain was Ramchand Parikh's marble. They refused to accept any payment but roti prepared by Sonia's hands. I, for my part, iodined their cuts, punched holes in crushed toenails to drain the blood, and gentled splinters out of hands rougher than brick. In return, they sawed and planed a cabinet for the upstairs room and whitewashed the balcony and side wall, which water damage had blotched bluish-grey the prior year.

The neighbours saw this unlikely friendship and decided I was totally lost. I enjoyed these mutual kindnesses with the workmen at first, but it soon felt like too much—as though I had fed stray puppies and now couldn't be rid of their loyalty.

The whispers of distaste should have been enough, but it took shouting to make us leave that neighbourhood for good. It happened shortly after Sonia told me she was pregnant. I overheard Ramchand Parikh arguing with his wife, Hema. They felt free to shout at each other because they did it in Gujarati and figured no one knew what they were saying. I knew enough Hindi to follow Gujarati. Hema was complaining about how tightfisted her husband was, how little money he let her spend. Ramchand pointed out all the things he was doing to the house—why wasn't she satisfied? Mention of the renovation brought out a new grievance. What use was this house, she escalated, when Ramchand made her leave it all day and stay at her sister's while the workers were here? Even at dusk, when they had the house back—the dust, the heaps of broken stone everywhere, there was nowhere to walk! Ramchand declared himself a strict husband, a husband who set rules and preserved the family honour—nothing like that Dr Jaitly, who let his wife hang around Muslims all day while he was at work, and was going to end up raising some bricklayer's bastard children.

PARTITIONS

. . .

Masud sits where he has been told. The policewallahs shuffle and deal the files out of file cabinets and scoot chairs and desks to separate sides of the room. Some of the pens do not have caps, so they take the caps off all the pens and distribute the caps and pens individually. Stamps are tested and classified by the dampness of their ink-pads; this is to keep India from slipping Pakistan the soon-to-be-useless ones, or vice versa. Careful tallies are kept of everything in the office. Every half-hour, they take a break and rip more pages out of ledgers. At around two in the afternoon, by the wall clock, they nap in chairs. Forty-five minutes later, both sets of heels slide off the desk and clap the floor sharply, and both men cough awake and pick at their eyes. They leave the chowki for afternoon tea. Not a glance towards his corner.

At half past three, they go back to work. This time they have brought boxes. They shuffle the loose papers upright and tap them against the desks, neat rectangles to go in the boxes. Masud waits. The sunlight through the door has crept across the floor and stretched trapezoidal against the far wall. A fly tickles his knuckle. Another fly tastes the sweat off his shaven cheek, which has darkened imperceptibly since morning. He rubs his face in both hands. It will be night soon. The city will slide out its carving knives.

The tearing has started up again. He stands and makes an anguished noise. The division has begun and will not stop until the whole book, whatever book it may be, is torn apart and meaningless, missing half of itself. Outside the chowki, the city, in late light, has darkened. Terror's intimate thumbs press his throat.

His chest strains upwards, trying to breathe. Cradling his doctor's bag against his chest, he turns in place, looking up at this gang of buildings that has encircled him. He takes off running, for nowhere at all.

Now it is time for my boys to leave, too.

When a second train approaches, they backstep off the track. Circling through the steam, they walk along the car windows, careful to hold hands as they do it. Every jostle tightens their grip by reflex. I walk behind them. Their bald spots are on opposite sides. Keshav's hair swirls clockwise, Shankar's goes counterclockwise, a mirror image. They have stopped calling for her. Now they just peer through the horizontal bars and move on. Sometimes still-youthful widows—unmistakable, black hair, white sarees— give them hope. It is never her.

I am with them the whole time. No matter how far I range, and I range far, my attention is on them. Habit makes me sidestep solid bodies. Trailing my boys today, though, in a crowd this thick, I stride through shoulders and luggage, as effortlessly disruptive as trampling a flower-patch. The living men I trespass on stop their sentences partway, forget their thoughts, or find themselves turning to my twins. The feeling lasts a moment, and then they recover their own concerns—I have passed. The women, more permeable, respond physiologically. Dizziness, a choking sensation, a flush. Bags and trunks don't change, but if they contain oil of any kind, I flash-freeze it opaque.

PARTITIONS

After the train leaves, the boys descend to the rails again and watch the crowd. They spend hours like this. No words pass between them. Hand in hand, their communication is direct. My twins converse through pulse rates, Morse-code squeezes, variations in palm heat and moisture.

Late afternoon. My boys' vigil is broken by the sound of screaming. The crowd on the platform panics. This is different from the nervous, shoving aggression that took over in the morning. This is the kind of stampede that has seen fire. Or a predator. Keshav and Shankar back away as the crowd pours over the platform. It's as if a glassed-off sea has shattered through. Spry men leap on to the tracks and receive their women. Sprained ankles yank the foot from the footfall as if the ground is on fire. Faster runners stick their hands between slower runners and widen their own way. Bodies erupt through bodies, the way smoke billows through smoke when a truck burns and the flame finds the fuel. My boys hug each other in this sudden thundercloud. Running risks stumbling, and stumbling means getting trampled. Standing still means someone is going to run into them and knock them to the ground. I kneel between the onrush and their small huddled bodies. I throw my arms out. But I am immaterial. I couldn't even block the seven hours' sunlight that has burned their cheeks and the backs of their necks.

What has happened? I divide myself. Now I am on the platform. There, near the entryway. Abandoned luggage marks a kind of blast radius. At the centre, three bodies. Their white clothes have been streaked a festival Holi red. The stabbing has been hasty, maybe some boys seeing what it was like. I bend close to the ground and see the faces disfigured in the manner of temple statuary, the tip of the nose missing. Proof of kill. There is money on offer in Lahore, as there was in Rawalpindi. I get back to my twins and urge them, shouting noiselessly, to start moving. Shankar tugs Keshav's hand and points down the track: east to India, and whatever waits along the way.

• Three •

Dispersal

Simran is a good daughter. I can see her, just two days ago, a full steel bucket in her hand, arm straight down, other arm straight out to compensate. At the edge of the bathroom tiles, she starts tipping it, not too much. The water feels its way around the squares. She squats and starts sweeping with a bound twig sheaf. A sweep, a tap, another sweep, another tap. She herds the water towards the open hole, its rim a pale green, calcine crust. From the lip of it she hooks a limp wad of her mother's thinning hair and sticks it to the wall, to throw out later. Old scums loosen into one murk. Afterwards, her footprints track the tiles dark.

Those prints lead to the kitchen, where she collects the dank, sour-milk-smelling cloth her mother uses to strain the yoghurt. Her mother likes her to wash it separately, out back where she does the dishes. A bar of coarse soap streaks and flecks the cloth maroon. Bunched in her hands, the cloth foams, but not much because the water is limestone-hard. Then she spreads it out and holds it before her. Its whiteness fills her vision and mine. She imagines snow—she has been curious, since she was a girl, about snow. I think of the antarpat held between a bride and groom during a wedding ceremony.

I imagine a Hindu ceremony, because it's the one I know—and because Sonia has wandered, again, into my mind. Staring at that white partition, I see what Sonia and I never had, married as we were to the drumming of a notary's stamp. It's something I never shared with her, but can conjure it more vividly, perhaps for that reason, than anything I have lived: Sonia with her nose pierced, heavy gold along the part in her hair; and the reds: sindoor, kumkum, saree, mouth. Intricate nets of brownish-orange mehndi up her forearms, my name hidden somewhere in it, her posture straight under all that jewellery . . . Simran lowers the cloth. She cannot see my face on the other side, just as I cannot see Sonia's.

Sonia . . . I am not looking there. I am *not* looking there.

I escape instead from Simran two days ago to Simran now. Climbing a tree reminded her of Jasbir, the way he would monkey into a high niche over her shouts and her mother's, his first quickest step vertical on the flat bark as he pulled his body towards it, forcing purchase. The next branches could have been ladder rungs until he straddled his chosen splay and grinned. She has abandoned him, she thinks. She has abandoned her mother and her sisters. From her eyes, I can tell she has been crying over this and is only now coming up for air.

The wind blows her chest icy. It blows across the place where she is wet from having held Priya. Held and dropped her: so much blood, so instantaneously, so everywhere. She looks down and flushes. Her thin white kameez is plastered to her, and her cold nipples show up dark through the bloodstain. No dupatta to cover them. Two tiny moles fleck her smooth, wheat-coloured bosom. She wishes, and wishes hard, that she could get rid of the body she has just saved. The way her father thought of her body—living deadweight slowing escape, a liability and an ostentation, inviting attack—is how she thinks of her body now, too.

PARTITIONS

Maybe this is just one more way Simran is a good daughter, willing herself to do her father's will. Her dominant concern, stashed in this tree, is how she might kill herself when she needs to. Periodically, her thinking drifts into fantasy—like living the rest of her life in this tree, brought berries by birds she would whistle to and train. The Mussulmaans would be so busy hunting Hindus and Sikhs on the ground, their torches would sweep and daggers slash well below her feet. Separated by a plane of glass, she might step on to it, watch them through it. And if their torchlit eyes flashed her way one night, she would widen her eyes, and they would think her an owl. Years would pass, her eating berries and keeping her mouth open overnight to get the same sprinkle of dew as the leaves, until finally, when everyone had gone quiet, she could go down and see if her village was still there, and if anyone remembered a girl, oh, about this tall, named Simran.

Will the Mussulmaans come to hunt in the mountains? They must know this is where the helpless ones would flee. The tenderer cuts of meat. They could find her at any time. She wants to come up with some way that will be quick and accessible in an emergency. How difficult, she thinks, how impossible it is to kill yourself in time, before the bad things happen to you! Besides a blade or a pistol, nothing works quickly enough. Even a blade would have to be used correctly—across the throat; she has heard of people dying with their throats slit. The throat would work. But would she be able to do it, if she had to? The body is so careful to protect its heart with ribs, everything vital inside a fortress. You can't enter without setting off pain, and the pain weakening your arm.

Well, then, I won't be weak, she decides. *I will do what Harpreet didn't, if I have to. I won't let a daughter of my father be turned into a Muslim.*

I search her a little and realize that, at her age, this is the worst she can imagine them doing to her. Conversion: it baffles me at first, but she has no way of truly understanding what those men would want with her. She has always been a religious girl, every ardaas by heart, songs, tales of martyrs she would tell her sisters before bed, stories about the persecuted Gurus. Conversion, in her mind, is lifelong captivity in forgetfulness. Everything she is, down to her name, replaced. She can't conceive how men can inflict worse than erasure. How the soul can suffer such a thing as defacement.

Every method she thinks of is imperfect, dangerous without being lethal. Killing is going on everywhere, but strip a body of metal and it is curiously powerless to harm itself decisively. She must leave this perch, if only to search the aftermath for a knife. Until then she would have to trust to God. She will stay close to cliffs, she thinks. Any ledge she can bolt for and throw herself off. Rivers might work, too, if fast enough. It's an inversion of the logic that keeps cautious sailors in sight of shore. Once she has a blade of some kind, she reasons, she will be safe, she will have an escape even if she can't run. The branches shake to either side as she braces where she climbed and eases herself on to the dim, sloped ground.

I know her sense of futility. I want hands the way her hands want a blade. Hands would equip me well enough for the violence I wish. Because the man I want to protect my boys from is skinny enough I could break him with half my former substance, thirty kilos would do it (I cast no great shadows when I lived). I see his gaunt frame and it puts me in mind of a hungry jackal, and I suspect that's what he was in his past life, or will be in his next. His name is Saif Nasir, and he is trailing my boys along the track, and has been for some time, ever since the tracks crossed Curzon Road and the boys stopped to stare at some bent bicycles and splintered carts.

The men—Saif had not been among them; he was the sort who watched—had shouldered their way into the traffic waiting for the train to pass, identified their targets, and grouped them on the side of the road. The people not selected—who still had one foot on their bicycle pedals, one on the road—held their poses, stiff, as if hounds were sniffing them. The crossing bars rose. The traffic started moving. The bodies fell. Saif trotted in later and found a ring. He checked the teeth but found no fillings; for striking gold, he carried a carpenter's chisel.

He has been listening.

Keshav. 'What do we do once we get to the next station?'

Shankar. 'We ask the stationmaster there.'

'Even if she did get off, how would he know?'

'She would go to him for help.'

'What if he doesn't know?'

'Then we go to the next station.'

It isn't hard for him to reconstruct what has happened. The boys are silent for a spell, and then they talk about Delhi, how Delhi will end up being their best chance—everyone who goes to India has to get their name written down in Delhi, right? If all the stations turn up nothing, they can ask at the 'big office'. That's the phrase they hold on to, the one they heard from Sonia earlier in the morning. We are going to Delhi, she had told them, to register at the big office and live in India. The big office—in the boys' minds, an immense building with khaki-uniformed chowki-dars and gardens and fountains, where all things are recorded and addressed in permanent English. The place from which the adult world derives its order and to which it reports. Delhi: they have an image of broad paved streets and cars and safety. They have not even seen a picture of it. All they have seen is their mother referring to Delhi as hope and end point. They cannot know the first thousand or so tents are being set up at Purana Qila. Crowds, like the ones they have watched all afternoon, wait to leave for Pakistan.

Saif whistles. It sounds somehow deft, agile, cunning to me, though there is nothing unusual about the sound. That whistle gives me the closest thing to sensation I have felt in years, a bris-tling, like hairs rising on the nape of my consciousness.

He whistles again. The twins, who are still holding hands, turn to him. Two long strides and he is beside the tracks, approaching.

'There you are,' he says. 'Do you know your mother has been

looking for you? Good thing she sent me out—she was worried you had left the station . . .'

Soon they are following him. It is an unfamiliar part of town, and nearly night. By the third turn, they wouldn't have been able to get back to the tracks, even if they broke away. Not that they want to break away—nor that the tracks offer anything more than an uninterrupted line between two fixed points in a broken, shifting country. He seems to know they are his now, and he walks ahead of them, casually, unafraid at the onset of dark. At one point he takes out his chisel and walks it along the bars of an abandoned bungalow's iron gate. Tap, tap, tap, he doesn't care who hears. His fearlessness, and the way he strides ahead, makes them shuffle to keep up. By staying close to him, they keep inside his radius of calmness, direction, certainty, and it draws them like a fire in the universal cold.

He starts whistling again and stops. 'The house is just over here. She's waiting to start dinner, you know.'

The house has a stone walk around the side, eucalyptus trees, and one pair of woman's sandals—not a pair they recognize as Sonia's—arranged, carefully parallel, beside the steps. The air smells of unfamiliar spices even at this remove. A single light burns within. Saif taps on the gate and flips the latch with the tip of his chisel. The boys step across the threshold. Dark shapes scatter off the terrace of the house, bats or small birds, no telling. Saif whistles.

There is the sound of a plate being set down. The light inside the house shakes and angles. Shankar takes a step forward, thinking it must be their mother. Keshav opens his mouth and loosens his hold on Shankar's hand, getting ready to shout recognition and run to her. Shankar takes back his foot and shifts closer to Keshav, who closes his mouth. The widow Shanaaz carries her oil lantern to the threshold. She likes to eat beside this intimate light, as she did when a girl—for everything else, bulbs and lamps will do. The twins see a small, benevolent face, lit by the lantern she raises to see them.

'See what I brought,' Saif says.

She doesn't answer him. Instead she walks the lantern closer and explores the boys' cuts, her face flickering, with the flame in the glass, through expressions of pain. Her face is unusually young and round, the hair thick though gray.

Keshav doesn't cringe from the soft hand that cups his face. The compassion, the grandmotherly tenderness, paralyses him. 'Where is our mother?' he asks.

'She's coming,' says the widow Shanaaz, and moves on to Shankar. His smaller face and body move her even more deeply. She looks to Saif, who is getting impatient, looking up at the night sky. Now, he knows, is when things will be getting started; the police must have leaked the list of neighbourhoods already. He needs to get hold of Qasim, and soon . . .

'How did this happen to them?' she asks. She turns back to Keshav, lantern brought close enough to the cut on his head that he can feel its heat. 'Poor children, you must be in so much pain! And look how brave you are, not a tear.'

'Lightly damaged. That is how I found them, Shanaaz bibi. Nothing that will leave a scar.'

Her voice, when she is dealing with Saif, takes on a haggling hardness, at odds with how she speaks to my twins. 'What will I do with two?'

'Shanaaz bibi, they are Hindu boys, clever Hindu boys. In two years, they will manage your money for you. You know how they are—wherever they go, the house fills up with gold. In ten years, I will come visit you in a new haveli, and then we'll talk.' He can tell she isn't persuaded, so he looks at the boys. 'Boy, what did your father do for a living?'

Keshav answers him.

Saif smiles at how well the gamble of posing the question has worked. His teeth show crooked, stained. The two front ones chipped sharp. 'Did you hear that? A doctor.'

The widow Shanaaz covers her mouth. 'Your father wasn't Dr Munshi, was he? The one who had his clinic near the old fort?'

Shankar shakes his head. Keshav declares, still more boldly, 'Our father was Dr Roshan Jaitly.'

Hearing my name in his voice dizzies me. This is the first time either son of mine has said my whole name out loud. I was gone before I could sound it out and have them repeat it. Sonia must have taught them.

'And your names?'

'Keshav.'

She nods and murmurs 'Qasif', as if she were repeating what he said. 'And yours?'

Shankar doesn't answer, worried, nervous about relinquishing his name.

'My brother's name is Shankar.'

The name is not as easy to revise to her liking. She pauses and strokes Shankar's cheek.

'How many years apart are you?'

'We're twins.' Keshav sounds almost angry. 'Can't you see?'

Saif Nasir laughs. The widow does not turn to him. 'When did you boys eat last?'

'Shanaaz bibi, it is getting late. Take them both for now. There are places that will take the one you don't want. I'll come back tomorrow morning. But before I go . . .'

She turns sharply and puts her finger to her lips. 'I'm bringing it, I'm bringing it.' Through the doorway, they see her lantern throw and stretch shadows, which jag across the wall and settle upright when she sets it flat. There is the scrape of a chest or safe pulled out from under a bed. I know Saif's mind. He is speculating how easy it would be to bludgeon the widow and take what is in her little trove as soon as she tugs the lock and slides it up and around and off . . . All his. Qasim would do it, maybe, with the city wild as it is. Not in more orderly times, and not in daylight. Saif prefers a transaction, prefers earning his money—either off a silly widow who wants a boy to spoil, or out of the mouths and pockets of the dead.

She counts him out the money, even though she has counted it once inside already. Her bad eyes squint at each note tilted to the lamplight. The boys watch, not understanding, in spite of what they have overheard. Saif holds his hand out patiently for each note, pockets them, and skips past the boys, rubbing Shankar's head. The gate's catch lowers behind them. The widow waves them in.

Nightfall. Simran listens to the darkness. How noisy the hot night is, insects clicking, shirring. But no shout, no crack, no crush of leaf. The only hint of her a burble in her stomach, and the realization, after she holds her breath to listen more closely, of how loudly she has been breathing. The milk had left a line of white where it touched her upper lip, still partly there in spite of her sleeve, but the afternoon sweat diluted and washed it away. That trace of tainted milk and her own salt are the closest thing to food or drink she has had all day.

Now that she is alone and in darkness, she sees, undistracted by earth and sky, what it is she has done. To have set off like this— where? To have detached herself. It's a kind of suicide. Leaving her family, she has left the caravan. Crowded city or empty desert were the same to a woman who had no family. That should have been the end, back there in the hot closed room, sleepy with morphine and scarcely registering the gunshot. Hadn't her father been merciful to drug them? The delay caused by that extra step had meant a risk to himself, what with the mobs so close. Only Simran had suspected, resisted, fled. And what would she have done if Priya had been with her? She has no way to feed herself, how would she have fed her little sister? Better to have ended there, her body useless to the crowd that kicked in the door. Slipping away as she has done, staying wide-eyed between dusk and dawn instead of sleeping between Jasbir and Priya, Simran fears she has outlived her own death.

She heads, almost by instinct, back to the starting point that should have been her end point. Something slimy gives way under her foot, mud or dung, no telling. She keeps the moon to her left and ducks, weakly, the snapback of branches her hand pushes blindly away. The first unexpected one slashes her cleanly across her right eye, but the lid closes in time. A sting across the forehead, a smart of the eye. Her hand cups that eyelid for some time. The terrain flattens. She stumbles more often than before, but eventually she finds her village lying in the moonlight, mute. A small cluster of dwellings, including her family's, still stands. A mosque. But the gurdwara's roof and one fallen wall fill the space where she used to worship. The Granth Sahib, somewhere under the rubble, makes no sound. Around their windows, where the fire spilled, the three remaining walls bear black stains. They make the windows look like punched eyes.

In the house, the bodies have been laid in a row and covered with white sheets. The men did this before they fled, with the drum sounding down the street and no time left. Priya has been moved here from the outer room. This is how the beast had found the bodies. The little the family owned is missing or broken, but only in the other rooms. In this room, nothing has been touched. Seeing them, the beast was cowed. It had turned away of its own.

One sheet covers three bodies, another covers two. She knows this by the number of dark spots on each. Her mother has been covered last, it seems, the sheet askew, tousled in places, her dusty feet showing. Simran straightens the sheet. She lays her own body next to her mother's. She will fit. The sheet, pulled past her forehead, cools her all over. The cloth on her back, after a second's delay, soaks through with blood, but it doesn't bother her. The floor itself is claiming her, absorbing her, fixing her in place. She sleeps the night as still and soundless as the others.

The twins have known nothing but kindness from women, and the widow reminds them of Haleema bibi, the midwife who had helped Sonia deliver and had never forgotten the family. After our move, she visited the house once or twice a year, bringing sweets, bouncing balls (identical in colour, so the boys wouldn't fight), the occasional kite. Her last visit had been in February; that March, she had coughed blood one night under a brown shawl. Come dawn, the muezzin could not wake her.

So when the widow soaps their scrapes, the boys let her. How can I resent the care she gives them? Her love has designs on them, her love wants to rename and reinvent them, yet her tenderness is no less real. The boys are puzzled but grateful. The only way she would treat them so kindly is if their mother told her to—she must really know their mother, or she must be a friend of Haleema bibi. 'Aati hai, aati hai,' is all the widow repeats when they ask her— she's coming, she's coming—so they keep checking the empty rooms and the empty street. Meanwhile the widow has them strip down, and their small chests flutter and fall, ribs visible, gooseflesh accentuated by the shadowy light. Shankar's side has a purplish-black stain that has spread to his armpit and around some way to his back. Her tongue clicks, and he buckles aside at her touch. Her touch is gentle, her singing steady, quiet, narcotic. Stacks of boys' shirts, freshly ironed, lie on the bed nearby. Keshav's is tight on him, but not Shankar's; Shankar is more the son she imagined when she purchased them. The shirts are years old. The smell of mothballs smarts on the air.

She sees Shankar eyeing his kameez, so she promises to mend, wash, and press their clothes tomorrow—and the washerwoman wouldn't touch such fine silk, never, the widow would soak and wring it by hand to make sure the colour didn't bleed . . . Were they hungry? Keshav says he doesn't want to start until their mother gets here.

The term he uses to address the widow, 'maasi', 'mother's sister', stops her short because it is so close to mother, it contains the word 'mother' inside it. The sound of that word in Keshav's mouth, the extra syllable so easy to chip away, shows her a future forming already, these boys *her* boys, coming home to *her*, eating the food of her hands. They would grow up to be brilliant—their fair skin and quick eyes and parentage and Hindu blood made that a certainty. She had enough to send one to England to study, and if she sold some of her gold, enough to send both. No young wife with her full womb would have a fuller home than the much-pitied Shanaaz, widowed at thirty-nine after proving barren an unbearable quarter-century, no prayer, no pilgrimage, no remedy enough. Once, on the recommendation of an Ayurvedic doctor

Munshi, she had eaten a mouthful of raw ashwagandha, which smelled of horse urine and rainfall over turned earth.

She sits them on the kitchen floor and gets two tawas going. They have eaten nothing all day. Simply breathing traps them there. The smells of flour, of cumin. Strange other smells, none of them wholly unappetizing. Soon she is clipping tongs on a pan and dropping the roti on to raw flame, that final drop that swells it with steam. Snatching it by the edge, she glistens it with ghee and folds it. Her hands do not mind the heat. Two mouths wait. It's as though she calls on two more arms. She had not expected Saif to deliver so early. The mutton and dahl, which she prepared for herself, fills their plates. The ladle doesn't come up half empty. It doesn't even tap the side or bottom of the pot. *How natural this feels*, she thinks. *Providing, feeding. So this is the magic that endows mothers! Two hungry boys tonight, and I didn't expect them, and everything is sufficient, the dough, the lamb, me.*

Keshav pauses before he pinches a bite. Shankar, always the hungrier, puts a cube in his mouth. It doesn't give like paneer. It doesn't cleave and crush like potato. He chews but doesn't make much progress. It has a stringy, gritty, resilient texture—and yet it gives out its own juice, as if it were a fruit.

'What's wrong, beta? Did you get a clove?'

Shankar shakes his head.

'A bone?'

He leans forward. The mouthful drops into his palm. The curry is off it, inside him now. The morsel itself, shredded, is greyish yellow. Her flour-pale hand strokes his head and slides away the plate. She scrapes the lamb back into the pot.

'You will get a taste for it, in time. A good Brahmin boy, of course. Our food is dirty, dirty. There's nothing in the dahl, beta. The dahl you can eat.'

He spoons it twice to appease her. The widow goes on making her rotis, but some of the joy has gone out of it. Shankar wishes he had not refused her food, but wouldn't it have been worse if he'd vomited? He fears he has endangered himself and his brother; her puzzling hospitality feels, all of a sudden, like captivity. He wants to get back to the train tracks. He wants to keep looking for his mother, who, he suspects, isn't coming here at all, but his legs are locked under him.

Keshav, reassured, bends forward and scoops his dahl makhni. A small black lentil-peel sticks to his lower lip. 'The dahl is okay, bhaiyya,' he says, and Shankar wants to stop him from eating so freely here, as if it might commit them to this house irrevocably. It's a difference I noticed even when they were toddlers: Shankar always worried, hesitant around strangers, moving water, ledges of any height; Keshav, meanwhile, all trust, extending arms whenever arms were extended to him. Trust is a reflex with Keshav.

The thin mattresses in the next room smell stale, and dust dims the lantern when she unfolds them, dust either blown off the floor or thumped from the mattress itself. The settling sheet swells and exhales mothball-breath. Her lies are more and more half-hearted. *Your mother will be waiting for you at dawn. Your mother wants you to get a night's sleep before she fetches you tomorrow.* The boys say nothing, her food heavy in their bellies, sleep heavy on their eyes. Lullabies she has practised every morning while bathing, her rhythm each cupful's splash over her shoul-

der, immobilize the boys further, like spells. This gentle inflex-
ibility, these reassurances—the boys can't read their situation.
They lie down parallel, docile, as if drugged, and they stare at the
ceiling. Meanwhile, she padlocks the door from the inside, slips
the key between her breasts, and snuffs the lantern. Moonlight
takes over, and the crickets seem to grow louder in the new darkness. The widow nestles her immense softness between them
and throws an arm across her eyes. Soon she is louder than the
crickets, snoring.

Morning. I am in the sky again. I take in the kafilas. They are
broader than I last remember. Great human rivers, the vanished
Sarasvati reborn with all her tributaries. My mind bobs on those
slow rivers, a paper boat. The one I want trickles east–west.
Migrant field hands who walked one way to eat now walk the
other way to starve. Craftsmen have left their workbenches tipped
over, as if whoever had been working there sprang to his feet at a
klaxon's sound. Drill or brush or awl is laid beside unsanded wood.
Most are villagers, of course, farmers in turbans, danda across
the shoulders, forearms perched on it and the hands slack at the
wrist. A casual, herder's pose, when they're the ones being herded.
The way they stare at the ground shows the difference: such men
usually turn their heads up to the clouds. I see one turn to face a
suspicious shake in the roadside brush, danda slid around, both
hands on it, ready if . . . Nothing. A boar, maybe. Or sparrows
mating.

On the road with these villagers, a stooped, gentlemanly figure, keeps pace. He seems dropped here by accident. A grime-collared button-down, no turban on his balding head. His scuffed doctor's bag makes him look as if he has strayed on a house call.

Morning. At precisely this early hour, Masud has done the same one thing for decades. A familiar pang starts low and in front—he knows, from studies and experience, this is where rectal distension sends its pain. His body has not forgotten.

Dozens of people, adults and children, squat by the roadside. They leave behind coils off-green or strangely bright brown without so much as the stray dog's kickback of dust. Masud has seen this his whole life yet never been part of it. Background and foreground shift, his vision bringing out these low human shrubs, unaware of themselves, sometimes even meeting his eyes, without shame. The women do it there, too, sarees bunched at their sides, because it would be risky to venture far from the kafila. Hunters wait in the fields; he heard them in the night and kept walking. A shout prematurely muffled, the snatching of the slowest, the smallest, the lame . . . A few steps out, and he gets a falling feeling. Each kafila negotiates a narrow ridge between abyss and abyss. The fields to each side are deceptively flat, deceptively solid.

What will he do for paper? Everywhere he looks is dust and twisted stem. His hand leaves off holding his stomach and brings the answer out of his black bag. The pharmacopoeia. The book falls open along a crease of much use—children's laxative tinctures and stool softeners, magnesium, sennakot, oil. One of the commonest problems a paediatrician sees, natural enough for the book to splay there. Two pages thumb effortlessly off the binding's gum. He looks ahead, looks over his shoulder, flushes. He drifts a little further off the dirt road, where he slows and stops, afraid to continue. Privacy is possible out there, if he ventures far enough. It will mean absolute vulnerability—not even the glass armour of another's witness, which is all the kafila can provide. He must do it here. He sets his black bag at his feet and unbuckles his belt. He cannot face the crowds behind him, as the other do. Even the empty field embarrasses him. As he squats, elbows clipping his shirt tails, he holds the two small pages over his eyes like the black bar of anonymity in a medical photograph, the infirmity naked beneath.

Morning. Simran is picking out a knife. She has used all of these, she knows their virtues and shortcomings. This slender one, due for sharpening, tapped at coriander and slid through bananas when Jasbir wanted them in sugar and milk. This one, serried, sawed at radish and potato, good, too, for taking the nubs off okra, leaving that watery mucus on her fingertips. And this one. The one for meat.

She takes them all, even the finger-length one with the green plastic handle. It had of all the knives drawn her blood most often, its sharpness so easily underestimated.

Her long back is soaked red, her kameez one bloodstain. She could change clothes. She could even bathe; a bucket of yesterday morning's water sits out back, flecked black. A single curved green leaf hovers among reflected clouds. Cleaning up doesn't occur to her. Instead she tucks away the knives. Her lips are moving. I catch scattered words of what I can tell is a prayer. She is already growing sure of her escape route. All she has to do is get to Amritsar. Once she gets to the Golden Temple, she will find work on the grounds. She will live alone, unmarried. She will work and pray and pray through her work. Hadn't she daydreamed about just such a thing, whenever her mother and father talked about giving her to a husband? Already Amritsar has given her purpose and quickened her movements. It's the same way that my boys fixated on Delhi, and for the same reason. As if in such times there were still safety in numbers. These city names are calming mantras, arbitrary fixed points, words imagined into refuges. They could just as well have said heaven.

Simran emerges from her house, crusted maroon with dried clots and armed, two knives ingeniously looped in her drawstring, two others wrapped in cloth and tucked in her waistband. The whole time she is murmuring, and her free hand carries a string of prayer beads.

The village has recovered overnight, the prior day's violence a late-autumn storm, a gang that blew through. Clear skies today, everything has had time to dry. It startles her how the routines hold exactly, minus the two dozen Sikhs murdered the previous day. Forty-year-old Rahmat Ali still loiters under the tree at the hub of the village, on his back, left calf splayed against right knee, tobacco spit streaking the dust to his side. When he looks up, he seems to be talking to the leaves, but really he is talking to Taqt Ali, his brother, several feet away, hammering shoe leather.

He lays off his work to stare at her as she passes. She is enough of a sight that even Rahmat Ali sits up. Either man could have taken her and kept her for himself—Taqt Ali might have gifted her to his brother, as some ancient ghazi would a distributed slave girl, the ancestral power relationships restored. Because Rahmat did need a wife. Even yesterday, during the action, he had shown his customary laziness. They had been to three villages; there had been plenty of girls, starting at twelve, but he hadn't liked any.

'Is that Jaswant Kaur's girl?'

'It is.'

The brothers don't touch her, and neither does anyone else. No one comes after her. In an hour, she is in the mountains again. Safe passage. At least this far. The villagers thought she had died with her family. No one had counted the shrouded bodies in the room; Taqt himself had bolted to chase down the men. The crowd had heard stories of faked deaths, and the blood, by their standards, didn't seem enough—so each corpse had got a few perfunctory pokes of steel. They see Simran and her dyed clothes and, though they are not by nature superstitious men, they believe their eyes. They believe she has risen. The story goes to the rest of the village and the villages surrounding, always the detail of the prayer beads, always the tone of awe.

Morning. The sparrows make their market-noise around the house of the widow Shanaaz. She is sleeping on her belly, one arm over Keshav's chest, one over Shankar's. It was a suffocating weight for some time, and they tried more than once, in the darkness, to set the arm aside and breathe. Shankar slid her arm almost to his neck so she wouldn't press on his ribcage. No matter how loudly she snored, she never seemed fully asleep. There was a startling shrewdness in the way her arm kept repositioning itself to make sure they could not leave. The boys stayed up late, speaking without voice, their moonlit raised hands making deft signals, like those of deaf children. In an hour, though, they fell asleep.

Not me. Throughout the night I poured thoughts into their minds. A little of that deluge soaked in, I hope. Even if they had stayed up and tried to leave, there was no way to slip out of that locked room, the key dropped where they could not fetch it, metal bars across the window.

The first thing Shanaaz does on waking is look to that window. Two sparrows perch on the bars. When they see her lift her head, they skip one skip and vanish.

In the improved light, she can see exactly what she purchased. She turns from one serene sleeping profile to the other, then brings her face up close and aligns it directly over Shankar's, which is tilted away from her. I rise protectively but cannot part them. I can see her, too, in this light. Her cleft chin and thick eyebrow make a profile nothing like my son's. She pauses there, filling with admiration and adoration. The imitation-love a kind-hearted stranger is capable of feeling for a beautiful child. Not love. Next is Keshav. I know the study she is making. I did it, too, in my last weeks. Hers is the effort to learn, mine was the effort to memorize. The kissing starts now, first gently and slowly, as she doesn't know how deeply they sleep. She switches between faces and sometimes between cheeks. Then, because they don't stir, her lips part a little and press harder and leave tiny glints of saliva. Her nose crushes to the side. Shankar's brow crinkles. He shifts, and his bewildered eyes open to the light. He blinks three times, frowning. Keshav, connected to him, awakens too. They are startled to see her and scoot away as they sit upright. Then Keshav senses the distance and hurries next to Shankar. They hold each other. Her smile pushes their backs flat against the wall.

'Hungry?'

They shake their heads. 'Where's our mother?' Keshav asks.

'She sent someone,' says the widow. Her morning breath fills the room. 'He came in the night. She had to go on to Delhi, to make sure everything is in order. She will send for you. Until then, she said, you must behave. Are you hungry, my babies?'

Shankar shakes his head. Her eyes lock on him and beam.

'No, no,' she murmurs. 'You are good Brahmin boys, you bathe at dawn, right? You always bathe in the morning, like a ritual. Come. We will bathe.'

The boys shake their heads.

'Don't worry, maasi will bathe you.'

She holds Shankar's wrist and with her other hand reaches for the key. She takes Shankar with her, already lifting his arm and tugging at the shirt. He snatches his arm back, and it vanishes up the sleeve. The shirt is already half off. Keshav follows, love his leash. They watch while she heats a pot full of water and pours it two inches high in an empty blue bucket. During the time it takes to heat, she rubs Shankar's naked back clockwise, pausing to trace the nicking of his spine. When she tongs the pot off the flame and focuses on the transfer, one hand still firmly on Shankar's wrist, Shankar looks at Keshav and makes a quick gesture and mouths, *Bhaag*. Run.

The water steams breathily into the bucket. Her attention is there. Keshav has a clear line to the front door and the daylight beyond it. He stays. So do I. We stay because we are family.

Now Shankar is in the bathroom. The tap thunders into the bucket. Shards of hot water sprinkle his hand. The widow blocks the doorway. She wants his drawstring. He looks down as her finger hooks his waistband, the knuckle hard against his stomach, and fishes for the loop. Where his feet touched the wet floor, he sees two dirt prints.

'Maasi,' he says.

'Speak, beta.'

The drawstring is out but not undone yet. She reaches past him to keep the bucket from overflowing.

'I saw a lizard, maasi.'

'Where? I'll clap my hands at him, and he'll run away.'

'In there. Behind the bucket.'

'Where?'

He points. She takes a step inside.

'I'll get him.' She smiles at his fear, plays along. 'Lizard? Where are you, Lizard?' She claps once. Another step. Twice. 'Lizard . . .'

As soon as she is through the door, Shankar slips past her to the other side of the door, pulls the door shut, and slides the latch, grinding it into its hole in the wall. The door starts shaking. An imprisoned, hollow voice calls to her babies, her baby boys, her precious ones. The shaking stops, and now a powerful blow rattles the door but doesn't shift the latch. A second, concentrated shock, louder: full body. A third. The hallway is empty, and the front door stands open. Shankar's wet footprints tell their escape. In the street, Keshav is checking over his shoulder, while Shankar is swimming up into his torn green silk kameez. When it slips on to him, his arms are left straight up, as if in victory.

Saif Nasir has had a busy night. He trailed two different gangs through the city, always trotting at a scavenger's distance from the feast. The take had been good; the second gang had been the best kind, randy and impatient and murderous, not one ring or earring stripped. Only the available necklace snatched and stuffed in the pocket, sometimes not even that. Every gang left its fingerprint, to his mind. A jackal can tell the pride from its scent on the leavings. The first gang, the one he abandoned after an hour, had begun to annoy him. The men had been vain, wanting to send messages, to humiliate—and that meant keeping the girls alive. Twice he had kneeled to peel a nostril back and unscrew the patch of a nose-ring when the girl twisted away and moaned. That was enough. A whole sack of trinkets and fillings sits knotted on his lap as he talks to Qasim.

'Have to get this to the goldsmith later this morning.'

'Who do you use?'

'I used to use Shah, the Hindu. But he left back in March,

when he found out our boys had him first on the list. Joined his brothers in East Africa.'

'I knew him. He was a real sisterfucking cheat, that Gujju.'

'They all are. Ours are no better. These days I go to Nasruddin.' He lifts the bag disinterestedly. 'I won't get as much as I did for those boys, though. That was great luck.'

'I had a lucky night, too. Look at this.'

Qasim pulls out a fob watch the size of his palm. A chain rustles free and swings, and he cups the chain with his other hand, brings it up and pours it like water into the hand with the fob. 'It still works,' he can't help but marvel. He has seen delicate things up close only after they have been broken. 'They worked on the man with sticks. Not one bone wasn't broken, I swear. A rich man, bungalow like an Angrez and the Angrezi gold fob, too. I felt around and found this thing in his breast pocket. Think how sturdy it must be.'

Qasim lets Saif hold it. Saif is jealous. Fake detachment in his voice, raising and lowering the watch on the scale of his hand, he says, 'Most of the weight is the gears, on the inside. Not gold. I could take it to Nasruddin, but you wouldn't get much.'

Qasim snatches back the prize. 'Who told you I wanted to melt it down?'

'Better to pawn it.'

Qasim shakes his head. 'This is staying in my pocket from now on. I am going to be rich as the fellow I took it from, soon enough. So rich I am going to need this to match my suits. I am through with foraging. This is Pakistan now, Saif. This is *ours*.'

'What, you plan to become a diplomat?'

They are sitting on the terrace of a house looted to the lintels. Their heels tap the wall and bounce and swing, like those of schoolboys. The city is a filthy spread, a table where others have finished eating. As if at sunset the people broke a fast and fell on it, knives out.

The money these days, Qasim explains, is in girls. 'In girls', he phrases it, the way a businessman might say 'in rice' or 'in shipping' or 'in gold'. They are everywhere, left unattended, needing only to be roped and put in a truck. No fathers, no brothers around, and if present, powerless ones, brainy little Hindus, toss a bloody shirt on the road and they turn and run, it's as good as a roadblock. Out in the country, he says, it's a free grab. None of this tugging trinkets off corpses, swollen fingers stubborn in the rings. Certain nawabs are paying three thousand rupees for each piece—Qasim uses the English word 'piece'—even though they know the supply is high; they want first choice, want to have the girls stood in a row so they can lift and squeeze a breast, thumb the lips up to check the teeth. Many of the girls were torn, marked up, but even the damaged ones were selling, though not to the zenanas. And it was clean work, just like what they were doing now. Yesterday Saif had been lucky to find those two boys, the smaller one almost exactly what the old widow wanted, but how often did Qasim get him tips like that? These girls are longing for someone to give them houses, chores, masters. They know their own men won't take them back. Seizing and selling them—it's a way of returning them to life. 'They'll be *thankful*.' Qasim grins at Saif and claps the muscled part between the neck and shoulder, squeezing roughly. 'And how do you think they'll thank us, hehn, brother?' Saif grins and lets himself be shaken; he has let that 'us' pass unquestioned. He is sold.

All Masud can think about is his hand. The pages lie crinkled behind him, spoor of a strange beast. His fingers fan and flex, fan and flex. The black bag he holds in his good hand. His attention is all on his soiled one. Don't let it touch the bag, don't let it touch his sleeve or trouser leg. It may well be a mercy to have this distraction. He has so much else to think about: his slit foot, for example, throbbing in the shoe. The tooth of hunger lodged in his abdomen. His dusting of ashes, his ruined clinic, his having nowhere to go.

An ox jingles behind him. He passes some coughing and a long, whistled wheeze, coming from behind a pile of bundles. The wheeze deepens echoingly into a rasp and spit. For a moment, he is reminded of a sick ward, and he begins thinking about what he must do here. Not in any willed way. His expression doesn't change. But I can sense the difference. He walks at a slight distance from the others, again unknowingly. Two steps aside, no more, but visibly an outlier, not entirely part of this kafila. His companions here are farmers, field hands and their families, who have many of them never seen a city. Sometimes he overhears conversations and cannot make out the words. Punjabi, Urdu, Farsi, English, he speaks them all. What sets him apart is their way of speaking, slurred, aspirated, full of contractions and hoarse elisions. The familiar made unfamiliar. Four decades of a paediatric practice haven't made him fluent in their speech. After all, not many patients came to him from the surrounding countryside. The parents rarely saw doctors themselves, so they were even less likely to bring a child in. The healthy children lived and joined them in the fields. The sick ones died.

As I watch him walk, I watch the walk itself. The gait. The others, too.

It reminds me of something my father once said when I was a boy. We were attending my youngest aunt's wedding. There was twenty-one years' difference between my father and her. My grandfather had remarried and continued fathering children into his late sixties. My father took us as a formality. This second lineage was never as close—a kind of mirror family with its own stories and cousin-clusters. Even the cuisine was unfamiliar. The patriarch had never had a taste for onion-stuffed naan before the second wife. Quiet politeness partitioned the two branches. It was somehow worse than being at a stranger's wedding. My siblings and I were a little wary of the step-cousins, who had already divided into their usual teams for cricket. One step-cousin chalked the wickets on a wall, another spun a washerwoman's bat. So we stuck together, and my father kept up a commentary. This was a treat. I remember the day because he didn't speak to us often. He told us how a good samosa needed more mirchi and less potato than this, how there were clouds to the east and the good weather might not last through the ceremony. And then he pointed at three men passing the tent.

'Mians. You can tell just from their walk,' he said, indicating them with his chin. Then he showed us, straightening his back and neck; I had never noticed his natural slouch before. 'Like lions.'

I studied them before they passed, his words showing me what I was seeing. Everything about them took on a different air, and the contrast with my relatives, dough-coloured and dough-soft, only confirmed it: they were harder than we were, fiercer, of one mind. Meat-eating warrior stock. No wonder they had come to this land as conquerors, sons of Mahmud of Ghazni and Muhammad of Ghor. They were, for the most part, poorer than we were, but there was something rough and masculine even about their poverty. Our yellow-gold rings and wrist-chains would not suit them. We Hindus, I thought, glancing at my Ganesha-bellied half-uncles—we were henpecked, bookish, slope-shouldered. No wonder our kingdoms fell to such fighters. Fighters they seemed by nature, forced to crank sugarcane juice and push carts. You could tell their true vocation, I thought, from their walk. 'Like lions.'

Compare Masud. Compare the twelve hundred or so Muslims to either side of him in this kafila. People scared for themselves and for their families, no prowess-of-Islam swagger. They were always one or the other, to my father: either a fearless master race, or the grandsons of pot-scrubbers who had converted to ingratiate themselves with some invading sultan. How little we knew each other, though for centuries our homes had shared walls. How little we will learn, now that all we share is a border.

PARTITIONS

. . .

Simran eats for what feels like the first time, finally far enough
from home to have an appetite. When the hunger comes, it's an
emergency. Khari biscuits from the kitchen's steel bin, one handful for the journey, flake her front. A mouthful sticks to the inside
of her cheek and stalls on the slope of her throat. She has no water
to wash them down in this land of five rivers. Still, she licks her
ring fingertip to collect the flakes one by one.

Her goal is Amritsar, but her feet wander. She stops and stares
at the tops of trees. Deep, trembling breaths. It may be the altitude, but it looks as if she were about to weep. She finds a spiral
road, and she walks it on the side of the drop. No rail, only the rare
kilometre marker, or a sign in English letters. At one point she is
faced with a metal fence and, overhead, thickly bundled, sagging
power lines. A sign meets her here, too, a black zigzag. Electricity
hums inside some low buildings, generating light for the cities of
the region. She looks in without comprehending, like a holy men-
dicant from a former century. A gatekeeper eyes her as she passes,
assuming, from the blood, that she is a cutting beggar, the kind
who would bury a cleaver in her own arm and wait by the shoes
outside a temple. Yet Simran has no wound to explain the blood
and no beggar's bowl. She moves on, no footprints behind her, no
words. Afterwards he finds it hard to remember her face.

A quarter-mile on, a bus surprises her. One moment isolation,
not one sense reporting to her mind. And then: thunder at face
level, dust and pebbles swirling around her, pinpricks, the brief
smell of heat and petrol. She shields her face with both arms, as

if against a blast, and stops walking. Through the dispersing dust, she makes out the whites of three passengers' eyes, their closed mouths. An older woman with her handbag close to her chest. One man in spectacles, one man in Freedom Fighter homespun. They stare at her through the receding window. The sight of her doesn't provoke a glance or murmur. They, too, are searching her for signs of the violence done to her. Are her clothes torn? Is her face cut? The blood makes them curious.

Feeling the inquisition of their looks, she decides she mustn't show herself this way. When the next vehicle approaches, this one a truck, she has been listening for it, and she slides herself a little down the side of the drop and waits. She likes having the drop so close to her. It comforts her, as the knives do.

Her hunger shrinks. Her eyes darken and sink into their sockets. The sun reddens her cheeks, an illusion of health. By noon, the ground, hours baking, hurts her feet. She tries to tear what she is wearing into strips to wrap them, but she isn't strong enough. Then her slowed mind remembers her knives, and she stabs and twists to start a rip. The cloth—its length enough to wrap once and knot, but not enough to wrap twice—is too thin to make a good sole. The long ends of the knots spill forward and tickle her. Within the hour, they have loosened a second time, and are good for one last swipe of sweat before they litter the roadside, tiny bloodstained scarves.

PARTITIONS

. . .

The twins don't run for long. Keshav could keep going. Shankar can't. His heart throws itself rhythmically against his throat. Its tip thumps far to the side, almost in line with his armpit, between the two lowest ribs. It makes the fractures pang in synchrony. His heart has ballooned over years of forcing blood through a pinched hose. Lips and palms grey, neck muscles straining to pull each breath, he calls to his brother and squats on the ground. Shankar has noticed this posture helps him, he doesn't know why; he learned to do it at around the same time he learned to run.

Keshav knows what has happened, so he doesn't tell his brother to keep running, even though they are still in sight of the widow's crow-crowded roof. Instead he runs back and helps him to the shade of a wall, out of the visible street, where Shankar drops into his squat again. Sonia never understood how far inside the defect lay, so she would massage Shankar's hands when they turned this way, as if to loosen them pink. Keshav does the same. Shankar nods. He still breathes hard. I keep an eye on the street while Keshav closes his hands on Shankar's closed hands. Prayer within prayer.

Let them have this breather. Dispersal is giving way to convergence. Clear across the city, Saif and Qasim have climbed into their truck. I hear the door shut; the window rolls down and Saif's elbow appears. They will be heading north. North of them, Simran walks so the afternoon sun is behind her. Over the next two hours, it will burn her neck. Masud, on the Indian side of the border, is coming directly towards her, across dozens of kilometres.

Masud's progress will be slow. He has heard a child suffering close by, and the sound, triggering a reflex, halts him. The tiny hairs along his ear rise, sentient antennae. He ventures out of the kafila and parts some branches to reveal a faint, insistent sobbing, where a boy of four or five holds his leg. Masud kneels. The bag's brass latch clicks open. It has been waiting.

· Four ·

Convergence

The three of them sit hip to hip in the cabin of the truck. Ayub, whose cousin in Rawalpindi owns the truck, has promised he will be the only one to drive it. Saif or Qasim or both could sit more comfortably in the cavernous, rattling hold of the truck, but that is where the girls will be bundled. Already it bears a female air, an air of subordination, not a place for men.

I watch as the truck heads north, driver's side to passenger window, Ayub, Qasim, Saif. A strange blankness in Ayub as he watches the road, eyes semi-focused at a middle distance. Thought and perception almost yogically overcome in the hypnosis of driving. Qasim is irked: he sits in the middle and envies the endless gust Saif faces with narrowed eyes. It was only natural that Qasim take the middle spot, as the connecting friend between Ayub and Saif. But after an hour squeezed here, he decides, they all know each other the same. He plans on pressing Saif to switch at the first stop. Saif, meanwhile, isn't enjoying the window seat, neither the wind nor the view. His mind is replaying Ayub's reaction when Qasim introduced Saif as their third man. The almost contemptuous glance at Saif's unhealthy-looking frame, about as fleshed-out as a bicycle's. Then the meeting of the eyes with Qasim, and Qasim's quick reassuring nod. Ayub says nothing to welcome Saif, and this rankles, too. He doesn't note how Ayub doesn't say much to Qasim, either, or how Ayub, surly and friendless, needed Qasim to find him his third. Ayub's only welcome, before they climbed in, was a breakdown of how the profits will be split: thirty per cent to Ayub, thirty per cent to Ayub's cousin whose truck this is, twenty per cent each to Qasim and Saif. Qasim seemed to have accepted the arrangement already, so Saif nodded. Though he knows he wasn't really in a position to haggle, he is angry over the mute docility of his nod. It must have confirmed, he thinks, Ayub's impression of his weakness. Saif wants to prove himself violent and masculine to Ayub, and he wants Qasim not to regret inviting him in on this. I see this eagerness intensify as we ride north, and it scares me.

Qasim, still irritated, picks at some dirty adhesive left over from the picture of Gayatri that had been taped to the dash. He scrapes off shreds and rolls them into a tiny ball. Just that week, the picture had been torn off and crushed and thrown out the window. The truck belonged to a rich grain merchant before Ayub's cousin took possession of it. The cousin wants to get the truck out of the area because he is worried order might be restored any day now, and all that has changed hands might be reclaimed and returned.

The truck has a Mercedes engine and space to carry ten, maybe fifteen girls. Any more might be hard for three men to herd. The girls are usually docile by the end of the ride and don't run, Ayub had heard, even if you let the ropes drop. They simply don't know *where* to run; the surroundings paralyse them. But Ayub wants to start his business right and has taken advice from the more seasoned hunter-gatherers in his tribe. What he needs, they have told him, is a Scheherazade. So he has hired a girl from Qasai Gali, who offers this other service. They stop in Rawalpindi before heading out.

PARTITIONS

The Scheherazade's name is Aisha, but the other girls, as they are boarded, will call her by a Hindu name, Kusum. Her voice confessionally breathless during the whole shuddering ride, Kusum will tell stories of what the girls' own families will do to them if they dare go home. Hiring her is their main initial expense, other than fuel and rope. Saif and Qasim have to pay in, forty per cent each. Ayub, who is providing the truck, sets these terms and covers the difference. It is too late to argue: Aisha's madam is waiting by Ayub's window, and Aisha's bedding has thumped into the back of the truck. The madam looks back and holds a finger up to Aisha, which tells her to wait until the counting has finished. When the madam is satisfied, Aisha climbs aboard.

These are the hours she usually sleeps, and her breathing slows even before Ayub shifts gear. Sleep deprivation switches her instantly into dream sleep. The potholes don't disturb her, nor do the rougher patches of road. I am happier back here with her than with the men up front, whose minds are colourless, cramped as the cabin they're sitting in. Aisha fascinates me because she has arrived at the same attitude towards her body as I have towards mine. She is oddly bodiless. The still-darkening bite marks on her right shoulder. The ache between her thighs. Her nipples chafed and gnawed, like a nursing mother's. She is as little aware of them awake as she is when asleep.

In her dream, she can sense things, but she never glimpses her own body. Her gaze floats free. Other people are pointing at sarees laid out on the sand or sipping water from green coconut shells. A kite-maker rubs glass shards on a thick bundle of kite-string. A few horses are led past on the shore, children given rides atop them. At some point, as a girl, she must have visited a shore. Now she is revisiting it, disembodied, as if after her own death, blessing all she sees. I can tell she is only observing her own dream—she has lost the habit of participating in her waking life, too. How close this is to how I am now. I dwell beside her a while. I stroke the long, wild blanket of her hair, let down six years ago and never tied back up.

The boys are lost. They have never been in this part of the city, and the part they know is nowhere near. After what happened, they don't trust adults enough to ask the way to the tracks. They are waiting to find someone closer to their age. Hope and instinct bid them turn at this street or that one. Sprints, of whatever distance Shankar can manage, take them down the quieter ones, but soon they are at the periphery of a populous square, looking at the backs of four police officers. They carry long rifles on their shoulders. Oil from the rifles has marked their white uniform shirts. They are watching something. Some kind of festival. My passage troubles the bidi smoke in front of a policewallah's face. Briefly, my own face's contours show, like a glass mask rising through water. Then I am gone.

A bear-sized Sikh named Prabhcharan is being held down in the square. Knees push in his back. Two men use both hands to secure his arms. Another man has thrown himself sideways over the lower back and beats, with what looks like a washerwoman's bat, the Sikh's hamstrings and the backs of his knees. I count four men and still they are having trouble. The pull on Prabhcharan's sleeves has torn his black kameez open, baring his dark-haired chest. This is not a straightforward murder—that would have been accomplished minutes ago. This is a subjugation and a show. The policewallahs maintain a supervisory distance, having received instructions not to help. One puts his pinkies to his mouth and whistles.

Prabhcharan roars and swings his left arm forward, then his right. The small men lose their holds and tumble, scraping pavement, but they spring to their feet. The Sikh has reared on to his knees, and his torso torques, one arm dislocated at his side, the other elbow high and reaching behind him, as if to pluck off a hooked bat. The third man, who slid off as Prabhcharan rose, now takes two-handed lumberjack-swings at a thigh. The other men are back; they run behind the Sikh and charge him as if he were a door, leading with their shoulders. The policewallah behind me picks the bidi from his mouth and shouts, '*Get on top of him, Ismail! Get on him!*' The whole tangle of bodies falls in a mound, the Sikh at the bottom of the pile, and a cheer goes up from the crowd. They begin to chant—'Kes, kes, kes'—and two more men come out of the crowd. Prabhcharan's body bucks and jerks under the weight of his attackers, but they have him pinned now, and the one on his back Vs his palms behind the Sikh's head, forcing it steady against the pavement. Now they are working at the turban. The thick knot comes loose. They extricate the cloth; it is passed on from where the work is being done and waved like a banner. A few children of three or four, understanding nothing, jump after the maroon cloth, snatching at it, a game with a prize. The hair is astonishingly long.

'What are they doing to him? Officer sahib! Save him!'

Keshav, get back!

The policewallah turns to Keshav with a look of murderous annoyance. Shankar emerges from the alley and pulls at his brother's arm. 'Haat!' spits the officer, the word used for stray dogs.

'But he's—'

Shankar tugs harder. The officer shows Keshav the back of his hand; if there were not so much to miss right now, he might have struck him.

Get back, son!

Keshav drifts with Shankar into the shelter of shadow. In the square, Prabhcharan roars again and forces a shoulder off the ground. A fist pounds it twice, flat. His face lifts, but the hair covers it. The chanting keeps up. A hand gathers his hair. Desperation makes him snap upward with his teeth. Ineffectual: the hair has been gathered, rope-thick, in a hand at his scalp, streaming and spreading beyond. They start crudely with a knife until someone runs scissors over. Swiftly now, in great swoops and snaps, the locks are cropped close to the scalp, some uneven patches, some patches pink and oozing where hair has been ripped outright. The beard is finished shortly. He is docile now and doesn't buck, as if all his strength had rested in his hair. A man walks a larger knife over. One hand cups Prabhcharan's chin and jerks back. His head tilts skywards unprotesting, eyes rolling white, throat bared.

PARTITIONS

. . .

It reminds me of Sonia combing her wet hair straight down, the comb leaving fine runnels. This must have been late, three months or so left—I remember the boys climbing on me, but I was still strong enough to lift Shankar straight up, my hands under his thighs, a throne. His tiny feet, smudged from the floor, dangled above my face, feet the focus of all genuine devotion. He stared around the room from this new height. She was combing her hair, and it got me noticing the boys' hair. It was splaying out over their ears. I pressed some of Keshav's between my index and middle fingers to show her how long it was. She nodded and said, 'They're getting stronger. It's harder and harder to hold them steady.'

Mightn't she try cutting their hair while they slept? It always came out uneven, she told me, as she couldn't turn on a proper light to work by; and worse, if she shifted them over to the opposite cheek, she risked waking them up halfway done, different lengths to either side of the part.

I was feeling stronger than usual, and I volunteered to hold them. I hobbled to the bathroom and sat shirtless, only the Brahmin thread across my chest. First Keshav, then Shankar. I kept a hand on both forearms and my legs ingeniously lotussed over his. My other hand secured his head against my chest, my rough old palm over soft cheeks and the tiny marble of a chin. It could have been a new yogic asana. How they cried! They had a terror of the scissors undiminished by Sonia's singing and my assurances. The crying ended only when I let them go.

Afterwards, smooth, black cuttings stuck to my shoulders and specked my white chest hair. The hair was wet, so wiping the cuttings off spread them into thin, individual clingers. I ended up bathing with the boys, something I rarely did. I was so short of breath by the middle of it that Sonia knotted her saree around her waist and took over. After a brisk soaping, each limb received two pours of the cup. She was systematic. I caught my breath on the bathroom floor, wheezing, drowning from the edema in my lungs. Still, I picked up Shankar to see his new haircut in the mirror. Our faces were next to each other. It could have been how the hair had diminished relative to the face, but his cheeks seemed fuller, pinker. I could have mistaken him for Keshav—the first time that was true. I appeared skeletal, my nose longer because of the sinkholes where my cheeks had been. I should have looked freshly bathed, but I looked instead as if I had run inside during a storm. Father and son.

That contrast, Shankar's face next to mine, made me grateful for the bargain I had made. I set him down and nodded at myself in the mirror. A nod of assurance and acceptance. *You saw for yourself. Everything has been taken care of. Now you live up to your end.* I returned to the cot that night coughing and spitting into a steel cup. Three months would have to pass before I rose from it. And not on my feet.

Masud is boiling two scalpels and a probe on a stranger's noon cookfire. He has lanced his sixth abscess of the morning and asked the use of this pot and water as recompense. Abscesses are every-where in the kafila. Every grit ripens a pearl of pus. Most are in the feet or legs from splinters, stray nails, thorns, scraping scrub. The only exceptions are the dog bites. And, of course, the human bites. Masud knows from medical school which bite is worse, which mouth fouler. The women always say it's a dog, as if there were any mistaking it. As if a dog would get that high, as if a dog would choose the place where the dip under the collarbone gives way to the breast's softness.

He has also braced a tibial fracture using sticks and a saree. He wasn't happy with his work, though. The skin had been broken. Had he been generous enough with the disinfectant? He had one dark glass bottle of iodine tincture in his bag, and its cap never failed to stain his fingers. A handful of bunched saree had muffled the open bottle, which he inverted quickly, righted, and capped, eager to conserve the solution, which coloured the saree purplish-brown. He had dabbed the skin, he hadn't really ster-ilized it. What if it got infected? What if the infection went to bone?

His instruments click and dance with the bubbles. Fifteen min-utes would be the proper duration, but the water will boil down before then. And the water he has asked for is precious to the family that let him have it. Already he has lanced a father's abscess and a son's, in succession, with only two flat wipes of the blade in between. Angular slashes of pink infected milkiness marked his sleeve, the forearm held up like a painter's palette.

The family is staring at him. A gentleman heron perfectly still against a background of shuffling migration. They don't realize how necessary this boiling is to what Masud wants to do. To them, it's just water wasted at hot high noon, and a longer delay on the roadside. He has treated their son, though, and they wish to pay him somehow. They figured he asked because he wanted to drink—he had jabbed his thumb at his upturned open mouth, after all, and nodded wildly when they said 'paani'. They never expected him to tear pages from his little book and resuscitate their dying cookfire, then set the pot on the hook and drop his instruments into the water. Or to smile so broadly when he saw, at last, the first tiny bubble.

Not that he isn't thirsty. His tongue feels swollen and his throat hurts, making it harder than usual to talk. Even the children need him to clear his throat and repeat things. Around the adults, if the child is somnolent or unconscious and cannot translate for him, he is all signs and nods. Masud hasn't had a sip of water for over a day now, and he doesn't plan to. At some point, he knows, the thirst will madden him, have him on his hands and knees lapping at heat-shimmer, but he doesn't trust the water. Even at home, he has always boiled his twice before drinking it, like a traveller.

The mother watches as he haemostats the pot and tips his shining hot scalpels into his bag. The bag is non-sterile on the inside, but he has lined it with the most rarely thumbed pages of his pharmacopoeia. She reaches into a bundle and pulls out two rotis, dry to the point that they snap when she folds them. Food he trusts more than water. Masud accepts her gift and joins his hands around them. 'Allah keep you,' she says, one hand on her son's feverish forehead. The other she raises to block the sun, which is directly behind Masud and follows him as he walks away.

PARTITIONS

. . .

The sun is not his only follower. I can see them keeping their distance, for now, but they have learned of him and whisper about him. The children. One, two, four, sixteen of them. As if his presence coaxes them out of hiding. The first boy he found on the roadside limps and watches him. He is an orphan, owning nothing but his rags and the big scythe-slash on his tiny thigh. He got it when his family took refuge with six others in a rice mill. The door became daylight, and the shouting outside became the shouting inside. He lay very still while it bled, the blood warm as a bedwetting. When he sat up, he was the only one who had been playing dead; he knew because he checked everyone else. His wound has been treated and dressed—under Masud's gauze, Masud's evenly spaced stitches. Other children gather, watching the old man curiously. They watch him slow down beside bodies wrecked in ditches. They watch him cup the heel and test an ankle or peel cloth from sticky, opened flesh. If there is nothing left to do, he closes the eyes. He struggles when there is no child he can talk to or talk through—marbles suddenly fill his mouth, and there's a pause and intake of breath before he starts again. The orphans have been there all along. It's only now that they choose to be seen. Any two communicate as wordlessly as twins.

One more follower. A thinly ribbed stray dog, brown with white patches and some patches of no fur at all. She hurries beside Masud, smelling somehow the brittle rotis, which are for all their staleness warm from the journey-long exposure. Her milk has swollen between her legs and swings with the trot, but no whelps trail her. A high-pitched note comes out of her throat, like the creaking of a cart.

'I hardly have enough for myself,' says Masud, easily. The dog cuts across to his other side and keeps pace. He takes a bite and chews to show her. 'There's nothing for you here. Haat!' The admonition is half-hearted. She can sense it; she has known the real thing. So she stops and lowers her nose to something imaginary on the ground, her interest seemingly diverted, and sure enough, he stops, too. 'I hardly have enough for myself.' A roti slaps the dust before her, and she gets to work without looking up, snapping up and sideways to manoeuvre it into place, as if it were meat.

The boys witness some things without entirely letting them in. Street, street corner, another street. Images emerge out of nothing, warp across the surfaces of their eyes, and return to nothing. The relationships of things are askew. The image that lodges in Keshav's mind is a young woman, four buildings away, stepping off a roof. She doesn't throw herself down, and she isn't pushed. It's deliberate, on to the ledge as on to the first step of a staircase, the next step the step off. As if she were a tightrope walker with the tightrope missing. Her falling is finished before he can point to it. The crowd of men beneath surges away from her landing, then closes back in on it. They remind me of still water reacting to a single raindrop.

PARTITIONS

The boys are so scared they don't even realize it when they pass through their own part of town. Three streets over is the place they've grown up, but nothing is familiar. In any case, our flat is about to change ownership: a lock-cutter has just clamped the lock Sonia left on it. The door jerks twice, and now there's the sound of the bolt sliding. It opens inwards. I stand in the doorway, the host. A man enters. I let him pass through me—just so they can feel a chill, a foreboding as they take this place over. He looks around and waves to the open door. Two women follow, and five children. The man goes out to bring up the bags. The children find the bin with the toys and start laying them on the floor. One of the women takes down my picture, along with the marigold garland Sonia strung around it—trash now, the picture and the flowers alike. The children have found Shankar's little damru and the stuffed monkey Keshav used to swing by the tail and launch at Lanka. The other woman sees the trunk open on my cot, holds up one of the shirts, and looks back at her sons. This trove of clothes will fit the younger one. She sits on the cot and starts weeping gratefully into the cloth. Meanwhile the man has brought up the fourth and last bundle. He goes into the kitchen where the russet pot still contains water and the steel cup sits inverted on the lid. He ladles himself a glass and drinks. His wives and children join him. He pours them each their draught of water until he has to tilt the pot to get the last. They have travelled a long distance. They, too, have given up a home, as I give up this one. They are all thirsty. The man inverts the earthen pot in both hands and shakes it over his open mouth.

. . .

It falls to Saif to unload the equipment. A casual order from Ayub to him sets up the hierarchy. Once Saif climbs in the back, where Aisha sits in her bedding and picks at her eye, there's no changing it, no matter how vigorously he pulls himself up by the hanging chain. He is third.

Ropes, rags, two axes, a long, flat knife. The corner of the truck is empty now. Saif sits down and scoots off the truck bed, overburdened, with one of the ropes trailing. He tries to tuck it back into its coil. Ayub draws it out, lets the loosened coil drop entirely, then loops it swiftly under and over, under and over his shoulder, impatient, fixing Saif's problem. They take what they want directly out of his arms and leave him with a frayed rope and the shorter axe. Aisha watches, and Saif doesn't like how this has happened in front of the woman. He can sense Qasim shifting, too. Qasim and Ayub walk side by side, and when Saif quicksteps ahead and places himself beside Qasim, he feels remote from the centre. He is reduced to eavesdropping on their strategy. Outright snatches are best saved for night, Ayub is saying—these are all things he has heard from practiced traffickers, but his voice sounds like experience. Even a night raid has blood in it, he warns, because families sleep close together, and some father or uncle, posted guard, may need his throat cut first. During the daytime, you look for the ones on the roadside who refuse to leave their husbands behind and sit there beating their chests. And there are always a few girls who have cut themselves from the herd, who slide away to tuck up their cholis and squat. No matter how dangerous the privacy, good girls, once they're at a bleeding age, just will not piss in front of their pappajis. 'You'll see, they go in pairs,' Ayub promises. 'For safety.'

The talk stops. Ayub has brought them to a sugarcane field. Stiff stalks part and close over them. From the kafila, their approach has the look of a wind. Not that anyone is looking at anything but the next footfall and the next. Close enough to hear axles creak, the three men crouch and watch. It is the long, patient contemplation of predators. Qasim and Saif wait for a signal, but the knife turns endlessly in Ayub's hand. His forearm muscles match his grinding jaw. Half an hour. Saif's hand recoils from his own hot neck. He senses the inaccessible sweetness all around him, locked in the cane, sugar locked away in splinter staves. Thirst. They exit the field the way they came. The place where they come out has changed, shifted like a shore. Ayub takes them one way, then, when nothing is familiar, the other. Finally they reach the truck, where Aisha has been sleeping the whole time, one knee in the air, one arm over her eyes, the same fly undetected now on her elbow, now on the round of her ring finger, now on her lip. Her fingers curl inwards passively, like the legs of a dead spider. Their voices make those fingers twitch to life. She sits up. Sure enough, they have come back towing no one. She is happy with the assignment so far. She could tell they were amateurs, and not just Saif.

A quick tear and chew of rotis. Soon they are out again. More than one family in the nearby kafila are using the late-afternoon light to stop and eat. I linger over two sisters a quarter-kilometre east. It happens exactly as Ayub conjectured it might, two girls going off a short distance, behind some scrub. A father and two brothers in earshot, but not looking directly their way. Two girls: Saif can tell immediately how it will happen, Ayub and Qasim coming away with their prizes, conquerors, and Saif, the third, doing at best some tying. He can imagine Ayub picking a knot loose and retying it correctly. So he puts his hand on Qasim's shoulder and points at his own chest, *me, I am going to do this*, then twists one of the rags into a taut gag. Ayub glances over, impressed at Saif's eagerness to spring, and, briefly, Saif senses himself dominant. Not second-in-command. The leader. That thought, by itself, strengthens him; he calls, as his prey, the taller, elder one. The sisters look around. Saif's is the first to lower herself. Without a cue to Ayub, Saif darts out of hiding.

The stretch snaps the overstrap of his left sandal. It flaps wildly, and his foot is bare by the second step. He stumbles, but he gets to the girl, tackles her clumsily and with his whole body. His focus is on her mouth and throat, shoving the rag with one hand, squeezing the throat with the other. Her teeth nick his knuckles. The rag has blood on it, but it isn't all his. He squirms atop her, increasingly panicky, far more sweat on his forehead and back than the exertion deserves. The rope comes alive in his hands and thrashes. Qasim brings his own rope and helps with the wrists. When Saif looks up, Ayub has the other sister over his shoulder, unconscious, long hair hanging past his waist. Neatly packaged. He checks in the direction of the girls' family, but even as he does so, he grins to watch Saif struggle. I sense both things at once, the apprehension and the amusement. Finally, after watching things a while, Ayub swings the younger sister forwards so the older one can see, and holds his blade parallel to the hair. It is enough.

Saif has to run her to the truck. He yanks her along by the hand. Qasim smirks at the sight of Saif and the girl like that, hand in hand. Saif changes his grip to her skinned elbow, which, though it leaves a red spot on his palm, looks more brutal, more proper. It's not the only place she has stained him—her urine splashed him at that first tackle, he is still bewildered by how much. The cloth is stuck to his stomach, just as wet there as it is on his back from sweat. The urine of near-dehydration, hers. I recognize it. Sharp in the nostrils, the colour of yellow gold.

When they get to the truck, Aisha raises the veil of hair over the unconscious one and clicks her tongue disapprovingly. 'These look like sisters.'

Ayub is interested in Aisha's opinions and advice, young though she is. She has seen how other, more practiced men do this. 'What's wrong with that?'

Aisha shrugs. 'That makes it hard.'

Ayub needs to hear no more. He pulls the rag out of the elder sister's mouth. Thumb and index finger spread her lips. 'This one's missing a tooth.'

Saif hides his hand. He doesn't want Ayub and Qasim seeing the gouge, between his first and second knuckles, deeper than the other teeth marks. The snatching was sloppy enough, and witnessed in full. They don't have to know that Saif damaged the piece, too.

Ayub, for his part, is keen-eyed enough to see the gum is still bleeding. He watches Aisha's reaction when he says, 'So we let this one go.'

Aisha scoots back and extends her arms for the younger

one, welcoming the body into the truck. As Ayub shuts the bay and Qasim stands up front beside the open passenger door (he wants the window this time, especially now that Saif is soiled), the sister realizes she is being left behind. Set free. Free to run back to her family, there to explain—what? How her sister was snatched, but she made it back? A sinkhole opens in her chest, deeper than any gunshot, which can, at its worst, go no further in than through and through. She and I are the only ones who feel it. Saif lets go of her elbow and wipes his hand, relieved not to haul this humiliation for the rest of the trip. Ayub rattles the keys and gets behind the wheel. The truck coughs. The girl lunges for the latch at the back, fingers scrabbling at it. Her thought isn't to break her sister out, which is what it looks like to Saif. She is already resigned to the spoliation. All she wants now is to stay with her sister. Not to let her wake up alone, or next to that girl, or under one of these men. To protect her from the one thing she can protect her from, which is being alone. Saif shoves her shoulder, but she falls back only a step. The truck starts inching ahead, and Qasim whistles sharply, walking beside it. Saif, humiliated again, shoves her a second time, pushing low and with a few steps' momentum, hands flat to her chest as if she were a man. This time he gets a better result. Ayub looks out the window as Saif climbs in wet and dusty and stinking, the only one on whom the expedition tells. Ayub's annoyance shows on the pedal after Qasim shuts the door. Saif hides his hands between his thighs. They ride in silence.

PARTITIONS

. . .

Simran, almost out of the mountains, laps at a stream on all fours. Distractedly, scarcely aware of what she is doing, she walks her palms into the water and lets her chest kiss the flow. The water, icy, shocks her breathing shallow. Downstream the water turns hazy pink as some of the old blood washes loose. She undoes her braid, and her fingers comb gummed blood into the stream. Rearing on her knees, she wrings it out. Wet hair, a long, straight rope of it, drapes her spine and trickles past the small of her back, gooseflesh everywhere. She heads back to the road. Not much traffic on it. Just one truck, miles away. But coming.

Masud never learns their true names. Only their nicknames. Dhimmy, Badshah, Rimzim, Jack. Street names from some forgotten city, their derivations lost: Lucky, short maybe for Luqman; Billi, 'cat', instead of Bilal. They are organized and tireless. Two scout ahead, two check up on those he has left behind. They note how far a skin infection's red has spread past the black border Masud has drawn around it, their measurements in fingerwidths. They jog up the kafila begging for water to boil, and on three occasions he finds a pot going, ready to sterilize his instruments. His bag itself cooperates, too. The tincture of iodine keeps pouring. The roll of gauze narrows far more slowly than it spins. The orphans find him lengths of clean, or at least clean-looking, cloth for tourniquets and bandages. Better cloth than what they wear. Pled from the living or scavenged off the dead, Masud doesn't ask.

Where he goes he goes as an entourage. The stray dogs have multiplied around him, drawn by scraps of the roti in which he is sporadically paid. He scatters small pieces like he's feeding ducks, ever-smaller shreds for ever-more numerous dogs. But they stick around even when he has no food to give them, quiet and well behaved, his irregular regiment. Only the occasional shrill scuffle and streak of infighting, usually at mealtime. When night falls and shouts wander the darkness, any torch that comes too close trips a havoc of barking. The dogs' necks strain and lengthen, their eyes glow back defiantly. For two hundred feet in both directions, the kafila is safe, and Masud, cheek on his black bag, sleeps in the eye of the maelstrom.

By night my boys have found the rail tracks again. They needed help, and help found them, peering down from a rooftop and hissing to get their attention. Her name was Maya Rani, and she slid a ladder down to them. It takes trust to climb a ladder offered—you are vulnerable during that hand-over-hand, foot-over-foot upward passage, and at the mercy of whomever let it down to you. They wouldn't have gone up if it hadn't been a child. She was three years older than them, though small for her age. The boys were drawn to her because her skin was as dark, and the same quality of dark, as their mother's.

'You're twins,' she said, delighted to see them side by side. 'I thought so.' Neither the assumption that Shankar was younger, nor the comment on their sizes: just twins, and she left it at that, and pulled the ladder hurriedly on to the terrace again, that brief perilous communication to the earth retracted. It felt safe up there, as if the terrace were a floating island and she had just drawn aboard the anchor. House fires brightened as dusk dimmed. The sparks they gave off grew bodies and became gangs with torches.

'What are you doing up here?' Shankar asked.

'Watching.' She gestured over the burning city. 'What were *you* doing down *there*?'

'We need to find our mother.'

'Isn't your father around?'

'No.'

'Mine isn't either. He never was.'

'Do you live here? In this house?'

'No.'

'Aren't you afraid to be up here, then?'

'Why would I be afraid? They come sometimes and shout at me. But no one dares touch me. Me or any of my friends. I haven't set foot on the ground for days. We jump from roof to roof, and all they can do is point up at the whites of our feet. No one dares come up and touch us.'

Her fearlessness was unusual enough, in that city, in that time, for the boys to credit her with some mysterious power. Keshav raised his hand and hovered it beside her bare arm. As though her dark skin were a candle from where he drew warmth. 'What happens?'

Maya laid her palm flat on her own arm and lifted it away. She did this twice. 'I don't know. They're just scared to touch me.'

'Can I?'

She held her arm out to them. On it my boys each rested a fair-skinned, soft, half-Brahmin hand. The contrast reminded me of their infancy, the contrast between their cheeks and Sonia's breasts as she cupped their soft skulls and cradled them aslant along her forearms.

'Did you feel anything?'

'Skin,' said Keshav.

'Skin,' agreed Shankar.

'Do you need to eat? The pots were still warm down there. They left in a rush, food still on the plates. One of the rotis was torn partway.'

'We ate last night.' Shankar looked at his feet. 'That was it.'

'Here.' Maya went to a coarse sack that had been a bag of durum once and still had the miller's stamp and weight in kilo-grammes. In it she kept a treasure of copper utensils, a salt shaker and a pepper shaker, and a full set of silverware, spoons stacked separately and bound by a string. No forks, she saw no use for forks—nothing they could poke that fingers couldn't grab more efficiently. Butter knives she had thrown in carelessly, and she took one out and smiled, using its dull edge to dimple her palm. 'What good is a knife like this? Look at my hand. Look. Doesn't cut anything. It's for show, like most things in these houses. They buy things and put things out just so other people can see. Only the kitchens have useful stuff.'

The boys kneeled to admire her trove, which she spread out.

A ladle, tongs slightly flame-discoloured at the pinch, a strainer. A steel rolling pin, heavy as a bludgeon—she had never seen one made of anything other than wood. A cylinder for churning out sev. And then, with a flourish, the grater. This one's sharpness she respected, and her voice lowered accordingly: she had sliced her thumb, she warned, just putting it in the bag.

'It's going to be a dowry. I already have enough for mine, though this sevi I might take. The rest is for my baby sister. Fifteen years from now, when she is ready, I'll take this out of a trunk and show her what I saved up for her. Who won't marry her then? She'll have whoever she wants.'

She skipped downstairs and brought up two plates heaped high with lukewarm food. I clapped my hands noiselessly: they had got full dinners, two nights in a row! I wished I could tell Sonia. She would be so relieved to know they were eating. But I am not looking at Sonia. The thought of her weakens my smile. I must not look there.

My boys fell to their food, not caring, as we had taught them not to care, who served it or who prepared it. The colour of hunger is fire, in every stomach the same. Before they started, she slid out one spoon gingerly and, with delicious ceremony, swirled their buttermilk's cumin sediment. While they ate, she stood and gazed out over the streets. It wasn't much of a vista, as the terrace wasn't that high off the ground, but she could see for two blocks in either direction, and it felt to her like a tower. Sometimes she giggled, and I looked where she was looking; the giggle meant she had seen a body beaten or stabbed.

'Do you want to stay up here with me?'

'We have to find our mother. We have to get to the railroad tracks.'

'The tracks? You're far away from the tracks.'

'We know.'

'It might be dangerous to walk down there. On the ground.'

'We have to get to the tracks and follow the tracks to Delhi.'

'To find our mother.'

Maya Rani nodded. Her trip downstairs this time brought back a silver case of kumkum, found at the foot of a framed picture of Gayatri. Dabbing her ring finger, she drew the boys a map, carefully to scale. On the terrace floor she traced crossroads the colour of blood. Round daubs meant a mosque or statue they could use as a landmark. But looking around at the darkness, she lost faith in her map. Her directions trailed off. Distractedly she rubbed the kumkum along the part in her hair, like a bride's sindoor, and said, 'It's night.'

'Is that where we turn?' Shankar insisted. His quick mind was memorizing her lines of kumkum black in the moonlight. 'At the mosque?'

'Come on. I'll take you.'

'But you said it isn't safe.'

'You can watch over us from up here, Maya Rani.'

'Come on.'

Simran has a hare's ear for trucks, and when this one comes, even though its lights aren't on in the twilight, she slides off the road and lets it pass. She is out of the mountains, and the trucks worry her more now that she doesn't have a comfortable abyss, only her arsenal of kitchen knives. She crouches in the brush, her back to an infinite flatness. The truck passes.

What she doesn't know is that this truck bears a cargo of eyes. Her figure is just visible to Aisha as Simran gets on to the road and continues walking. Unmistakably female. Unmistakably young. Aisha feels something like pity for the would-be abductors who have been driving her around the whole day. The trip started before noon and they have harvested only two girls. One is the sister, a twelve-year-old, still occasionally vomiting over the side—either from terror, or motion sickness, or the skull blow Ayub gave her. Between crying and vomiting, she has not been well enough even to share her name, in spite of Aisha's sisterly coaxing. Aisha had parted the girl's hair and found the whole back of her scalp purplish-black and swollen soft.

The second girl they brought back had been refuse—tattooed right across the forehead. *Good luck selling that one*, she thought when Ayub pushed her into the truck. No blow had been required. The girl, who said her name was Uma, had come along passively, used to being handled. I study Uma briefly and discover she is puzzled her three captors have not raped her yet. I follow her eyes to Aisha and the young girl. Uma assumes the men sated themselves on the other two earlier in the afternoon and will get to her later that night. The detachedness of her contemplation is unbearable to me. Every boundary demarcating her has been violated already. She is, body and mind, all one perforation. Nothing holds her in, nothing holds her together. Through all those holes and rents she has dispersed, though yet living. Neither the will to live nor the will to kill herself. No will at all. This is a state I had not thought possible. I am dead but not deadened; she is deadened but not dead. I pull away.

At Aisha's pounding, the truck stops. Ayub bolts out, thinking one of the girls has escaped. 'What happened?'

'Look. There.'

One girl motionless in the dark. One girl getting smaller.

Maya Rani has led my twins to the tracks, has toed the tracks like a river she dare not enter. And she has left. They keep waiting for her to find some stairwell, some ladder to the rooftops, where she is invincible. They want to see her fly from roof to roof in a flash of choli sewn with little discs of mirror, dark against the darkness, so they can be sure she is safe, untouchable. A fish of the air, altitude her water. But she walks until they cannot see her. Even after her vanishing, Keshav thinks he sees her, once, illuminated from the side by a distant fire. But he isn't sure, and neither am I. Because I am not following her. I don't even know where Masud is right now. He has his guardians. Simran and my twins are alone. I am all they have.

Simran doesn't even have herself. When the hands come for her, she holds a knife flush with her neck, a prayer on her lips. Yet the pose, even as she does it, changes its meaning. It becomes a threat, *any closer and I will kill myself, any closer, any closer and I swear*

I will . . . She threatens suicide in front of someone who doesn't consider her fully alive. It's not what she intended it to be, a glorious martyrdom, the pure Sikh virgin defying the predator Mussulmaan. It's just a threat with which her hand refuses to cooperate. Her hand resists like statuary. Her neck resists like leather. The point touches it, dimples it, but just won't slide through. I know the anatomy. Her jugular flutters under the knife. Half an inch in, and the cut will be sufficient for a steady, venous bleed. Not the jet of the carotid, nothing so dramatic—but the vein would bleed her out just as totally, a deliberate tipping of the cup until she is all poured. But the vein isn't going to bleed.

The struggle happens in the tail lights of the idling truck. Ayub's figure all silhouette, Simran's panic illuminated red. His fingers wrap her forearm at its middle and still close the circle. She realizes, all at once, how small she is. The female strength that could haul buckets from a well, or wipe the counter with her four-year-old brother chattering on her cocked, girlish hip, is not the same as male strength. Ayub's fat thumb presses down on the tendons of her wrist, and her fingers slacken, overridden. There is disdain in the slap with which he knocks the weapon from her hand. As if she has no right to one, not even one turned against herself. Then he walks her by the arm to the truck.

It is night. He has no way of knowing about the other knives. I can imagine her making her escape using those other knives, maybe even freeing the others, the rope sawed through and Aisha screaming. But Simran is thinking about her father and her family and swearing to them she is strong enough to stay pure. She must not fail. Her hand makes a grab for the two knives at her drawstring, but they tangle there and hold. Closer to the tail lights now, Ayub can see the shapes of the knives. His first flash feeling is fear—he had been helpless, his back turned to her—she could have stabbed him. Quickly it turns to rage. This dirty wandering Hindu girl (he thinks she is Hindu), just like their men, full of guile, hiding sly little knives all over.

Qasim and Saif have got down, their bared teeth and eyes gleefully white while Ayub strips Simran of her clothes. First the drawstring, which he uses the knife tangled in it to cut. His knife hand jumps when his sawing finally snaps through. Then he forces her head down and her arms over her head. She screams each time he pulls. The sleeves tear. Uma breaks a reverie and sits up straight, interested. Aisha has been watching from the beginning. The twelve-year-old girl, crescents of blood clot along the halves of her brain, is the only one of us not watching. Her pupils, under her half-open eyelids, are the size of the dots on a flown butterfly's wings. They think she is a sound sleeper.

Ayub shakes out Simran's arsenal. He holds the clothes up and aside like infestation, squeezes them looking for more knives. Then he throws them in the truck and looks at what he has found. The three stare at her in the red tail lights of the truck. Her arms are too thin to cover anything. No hiding herself. She spills out of her own embrace. She sinks to the ground. Ayub draws her to her feet by her braid. Once she is standing, he lays the braid on his palm. Hair converging on hair around more hair. His thumb and forefinger stroke its rainwater-down-a-kerb length, tracing it from her shoulder towards his heart. His fingertips catch on the band at the end and slide it off. Ayub spreads the braid slowly, lifting and setting aside each half until he has traced it back to her shoulder, past that to the back of her head. There, at the source of her black hair, his hand grips hard and holds her aloft like a rare bulb uprooted forever from the earth.

If it were up to Keshav, they would be running down the tracks right now, all the way home to the far point where the tracks converged. Hadn't they lost time at the station, then in the widow's house, then today's futile hours wandering the city? Keshav doesn't want to sleep. The first station they get to, a small one an hour away by foot, is still awake. Bug-flecked bulbs and a pair of cars locked in rust on a side track. It has nothing like the crowd of the main station downtown, maybe because of the late hour, maybe because more reports have been coming back of violence on the trains. Keshav points at the distant green signal. Shankar, seeing it, glances back immediately, searching for any pinpoint of light that will dilate into a train's eye.

If it were up to Shankar, too, they would be running. But Shankar's body, always separate from him, refuses. Shankar, smaller, has grown heavy all over. Simply walking feels to him like wading in floodwater. It's not the same loud, strained breathing he went into right after they ran from the widow's house. There's something shallow and noiseless about it that troubles my physician's ear, sensitive to pathology as a musician's is to dissonance. I crouch to his chest, the side where his bruise is. Broken ribs aren't lethal in themselves. They make for sharp, unrelenting, uncomplicated pain. Thorns in the side, not knives in the heart. In fact I used to be relieved, in the examination room, to discover a patient's chest pain had a button I could press—it meant I wasn't dealing with a heart attack.

The silky rustle of expanding and subsiding lung, though, has vanished on one side. This can mean only one thing: the lung has peeled off the inner surface of his chest. A physiological vacuum-seal is supposed to keep them flush. Break the ribs, sometimes you break the seal. The lung shrinks back on to its own bronchus. The diaphragm pulls in vain. The lung doesn't expand, or at least not as much as it's supposed to. That's what has happened with Shankar. It wasn't like that when he was first injured—I know because I listened there, out of reflex. When he slept beside the widow, too, I hadn't noticed anything. Over the past day, with the boys hurrying a stretch, dropping to their knees, peering around corners—it hasn't been quiet enough, until now, for me to hear him breathe. The lung could have dropped anywhere, at any minor provocation. A stumble, the pressure of Keshav's or Maya Rani's arm holding him close before the next dash, even the stresses from his own movements. A wince of pain there like the ones before it, and at first only a crescent of dead space around the lung. Now, after their cross-city trek to the tracks at night, there must be a half-inch or more.

He doesn't have reserves to begin with—no wonder he stops on the platform and waves Keshav on. Shankar squats, thinking it's the usual shortness of breath. His eyes go with Keshav. His brother first tries the ticket window, on tiptoe, hands on the ledge, calling inside. From his distance, Shankar can see that no one is in the chair, no one in the booth. Keshav glances at his brother, and Shankar shakes his head. I can see the sweat on his forehead under the electric tube light. The dull blue around his lips makes him look cold in this oven of a night. A chai wallah wipes the grit from his cups with the end of his shirt. Keshav goes up to him and explains, gestures up the tracks one way and then the other, Pakistan, India. The man takes a new patch of his shirt and gets to work on his saucers now, quick rotations. Keshav asks where the stationmaster is. The man pauses a second in his work, points at the clock on the wall, and wags his thumb. When Keshav starts describing Sonia, the chai wallah interrupts him. His hand juts at the other people on the platform, at the heavens. He goes back to his work. Keshav takes Shankar's hand and helps him rise. His brother takes short, shallow breaths, hand resting just below his throat, the sound of it like sobbing.

More stations. The night doesn't get any cooler, nor Shankar's breathing any easier, no matter how often he folds his knees to his chest. The squat, though he doesn't know it, has a specific mechanism: it kinks the arteries to his legs, so the blood that's supposed to go from his heart to his body goes, instead, to his lungs. Part of his 'blue disease' is a hole between the right and left chambers of his heart—that muscular partition, imperfect. Squatting like

this can force blood through it, get more blood to his lungs, to be loaded up with oxygen.

What's wrong now, though, is wrong with the lung itself. So squatting will not ease things for him. There's no way for him to know that, so he does it every half-kilometre or so. Keshav rubs his brother's back as though helping him cough. The coughs, when they do come, skip into breathlessness, like something trying to get purchase but slipping. And yet the distance gets walked—he is strong. He has always been strong.

They learn not to expect help. They learn to look for themselves and move on. Shankar uses each arrival as respite while Keshav checks each bench and circles each pillar. It's like ringing every bell in the circuit of a temple, a precise, prescribed rite. He calls to her at the abandoned ticket desk, calls to her beside the station name painted in block English letters, calls to her over the empty tracks. Then he returns to Shankar, and they walk on either side of the rails, ball of a foot on every other slat, looking down. Shankar counts steps in his head to concentrate on something other than the vise he breathes against. I have seen this whole time how their steps are synchronized. At one point they notice it, too; in an absurd interval of playfulness, they switch up their steps, a pause, a reverse step, a wag of the foot, rejoicing in how they cannot escape each other, every spontaneous variation matched, a mirror image. For an absurd interval, they are both smiling, Keshav laughing, Shankar giggling noiselessly through his fractures, only his mouth open. He still thinks this is one of his spells, and he is used to Keshav making him laugh during his spells—the squat is, as Keshav likes to grimace, the same position people take over the latrine. There on the moonlit tracks, the three of us laugh a laughter that doesn't have any happiness in it. It's the same kind of mirth that sometimes shakes funeral-goers. We stop only when Shankar lowers himself again, hand up, as if he wants a break before laughing again. His breaths stretch into long, shrill draws, nostrils flared. He and Keshav look in each other's eyes. Shankar steadies himself and stands.

The next station is a small one, just two slabs and two awnings. Many of the larger expresses don't even stop there, but this night, a long train is at the platform. For no reason at all, they start to hope. It looks like the same train to them. It isn't, of course, and in any case, it is facing them, heading the wrong way. The boys hurry, Shankar's hand in Keshav's. They are already close when I realize something is off. Most of the train's length doesn't line up along the platform's, only the first car's. Not one light is on in the station, small though it is. One fixture, I can see, hasn't finished swinging. The main signal light, facing down the track, should be red, but Keshav almost cuts his foot on its shards. He guides Shankar clear. No one is on the roof of the train. No voices in any compartment. The boys approach the engine car. No driver. The corner of the first passenger car, immediately behind it, drips a dark oil.

'It broke down,' Keshav whispers, pointing at the ground, where the oil has pooled. He touches the oil and rubs it between his fingers. It is thinner than he expected, and rubs clear. He smells it.

Shankar grabs his brother's hand and points down the track. Every car drips its own black puddle. Because just across the border that night, on a crowded platform, sixteen men sat meditating,

beards on their chests, swords across their knees. Simran's cousin
Harpreet had been among them. The people around them knew the
object of their meditation and watched at a distance. The stationmaster, staring at their bowed turbans, changed the signal to clear
the train's arrival. The men stood in the rising steam and vanished.

Keshav backs away from the blood and wipes his fingers on his
shirt. He holds his strangely throbbing fingertips for the next half-
hour, as if he has been cut. As if the blood were his.

Masud's sleep is precious to his entourage, as precious as the sleeper
himself. The orphans lie nearby, interspersed among the strays.
They sleep in shifts, like sentries. The ones who stay awake discuss him. This kafila, like any kafila, ends in a city, a camp. They
decide they must get him there. He must survive. All through the
night there are families still walking past, leading drowsy mules or
pushing rickety-axled carts. The orphans wait for the right one, a
solitary old farmer too scared to stop driving his ox cart. The cart
is piled with clothes, one bundle of pots and pans, and one body,
his wife's. The children pour themselves across his way. He snaps
his whip at them and shouts. The strays wake up vociferously and
want in on the skirmish, but Lucky, the talker, offers the whip his
arm and lets it coil around. The farmer shakes it free. The second
time it spirals up Lucky's arm, he grabs it and explains.

Masud, disoriented, has sat up; he rubs his eyes, face in
his hands like a weeping man. He is malleable, guided by the

children, who reach up to lead him by his elbows. Billi brings the black bag in both hands, and they set him down snugly, cushioned with clothes. Beside the corpse of the woman, whom he never sees, he falls asleep again.

The farmer's first reaction had been resistance. That was to be expected. Lucky's explanation stopped him short, though. When he saw how tenderly the children preserved this old man, he thought of his own grandchildren, in his daughter's village. Whether they were alive tonight, and, if so, where. The sight of kindness reminded him of a lost, golden past, before the invention of borders, when kindness was possible. Prehistory just last year. So he let this extra cargo on to his cart, and even leaned over to help move his wife's body closer to himself. Then he clicked his tongue, and the cart clopped creakingly towards Pakistan, accompanied by an alertly trotting escort. Masud rocked on his side, hands joined under his cheek.

• Five •

Arrivals

Masud wakes up on the cart and squints into the late-morning light, his back aching and half his face finely printed by the leather of his black bag. At some point in the night, he shifted it from belly level, where Billi had nestled it, to under his cheek. Yesterday's interrupted shave has given his face a split shading, dark scruff on one side, darker beard on the other. Now, on his paler side, this network of intricate lines seems to have aged him more swiftly.

A bewildered glance infers nothing from his driver's back. The small body, wrapped in a white sheet, seems shaped like a woman's, and he assumes she is sleeping. The only things that reassure him are the strays, who aren't alarmed. None of them are looking his way. One, low to the ground, trails an olfactory hunch off the road. Masud scoots off and lets the cart go on without him. The farmer senses the cart shake and lighten, and he looks over his shoulder to make sure nothing has fallen. He sees the doctor standing in the road, dogs calmly sniffing circles around him, and he raises a hand. Masud, still uncertain what has happened, raises his hand in answer.

He doesn't know it, but he is almost at the border. Only two hours, at his rate of walking, from the closest camp. He never knows when he crosses the border. It is too early in the border's life cycle: it hasn't budded checkpoints and manned booths yet, hasn't sprouted its barbed-wire thorns.

He could get to the camp before noon, if all he does is walk. Lucky and Rimzim, who have kept up with the cart on foot all night, come running with summaries of the cases up the road. Two hours stretch to four. They have picked up the skills quickly, having attended dozens of examinations the prior day; Masud's questions, around the adult patients, were often posed directly to them. So they collect the information they know he will need, where is the pain, how long has it been going on, is it dull or sharp or throbbing. Or, as is more often the case, where did they cut you, when did they cut you, what did they cut you with. The first patient he treats that morning is Lucky. Spiral whip welts wrap his forearm like two snakes up a caduceus.

I follow Masud into the camp. Here, too, there is no physical boundary. No sign, no appreciable transition. It forms itself gradually, like a city approached from the countryside. First the outskirts. Huddles of people, human shanties. Then, as he walks further, he passes a gradual scatter of tents. Or not tents exactly, but staked and propped lengths of burlap or saree. Under that richly coloured shade, large-eyed hunted mammals cower and peer up at him. The tents get closer together, and then, by an orderly dereliction, corridors define themselves. He can look down them for hundreds of yards. He can stand at their intersections. Streets of a miniature city, complete with human sewage dropped as indifferently as cow dung. The camp. Pakistan.

His strays have dispersed—other dogs are already established here, the tripwires of their urine everywhere. Negotiations, alliances, skirmishes growl and yelp sporadically across the camp. These, too, are questions of borders, jurisdiction, rights of access.

PARTITIONS

The first voice Masud hears is that of a man named Maulana Ijaz. The maulana is dressed in austere white and a knit cap, a dramatic grey beard down his front. A metal trunk lies open at his feet. His eyes have rolled back, and his neck is tucked very low between his shoulders, while his face is turned directly to the sun. His hands betray his blindness as he lowers tentatively and flutters his fingers over the contents of a trunk. He brings up a small skull.

'Look, O brothers,' he says, 'look!' His whole body is stretched to get the skull as high as possible. He sways as one stalk, the skull a seed-pod he wants the winds to take. 'This is what they are doing to us, to our sons! They know our boys will never lower their heads. They pull us into the street and say, "Spit on your Qur'an," but we won't do it. This child, he was a warrior to the end, and handsome, a Pathan boy, green eyes. A little man. You should have heard him shout. So this is what they did. This proud boy, ya Allah, if only they had taken my eyes before then, I wouldn't have had to see it. Do you see, O Muslims? Do you see what Hindustan plans for our sons?'

Masud squints at the skull. There is something wrong with it. The back of the skull balloons out, and the eye sockets are too large. Masud angles his head, studying it.

The maulana hands the skull to the person nearest him, and it passes from hand to hand. He descends to his trunk again and this time comes up with a stack of six photographs, each in a plastic slipcover. 'But it's our daughters they have always been after. These pure girls had no one to protect them. Do not cover your eyes. Look. Look at what has been done to them.' The photographs are handed off, too. 'One look and pass them on, make sure everyone gets a chance to see,' the maulana adds quietly, in his speaking voice. Now he switches back into his strident, public voice. 'No one to protect them—but tell me, believers, do they have anyone to avenge them? What, will no one avenge them?'

He lowers his face from the sun. The crowd remains a silent semicircle. The skull makes it to Masud. The jaw is lost; he offers his flat palm, and the maxilla rests on it, top molars biting him. He holds it only for the time it takes to pass it to the man next to him. Long enough for him to be certain the skull is no human child's. The maulana starts up again, his blind eyes tearing up, and Masud realizes there is sincerity here, in spite of the circus-crier shrillness and the exhortations that come now. Maybe the maulana doesn't even know he shows his congregation—his audience—a monkey's skull. Maybe he does.

Masud drifts away before the photographs make it to him. He has seen the bite marks up close. His scalpel, just the prior day, traced the abscessed letters where a man had knifed his name. The word split and oozed as Masud's blade followed the previous blade's track.

I know what bothers him about this, why he cannot bear the calls to vengeance, redemption, war: Masud can bear to see the suffering, but he cannot bear to see it presented. The maulana is recruiting. I see for the first time the young men behind him. Two Pathans. They have been taking the maulana around the camp, calling crowds together to watch his show. They have collected fighters to join up and ride out. They call themselves 'ghazis', frontier warriors, what the first Muslims called themselves when they galloped as far as Sindh. Masud doesn't see the past and future around this display, but he senses as much, and he cannot tolerate a reason behind speaking or showing other than compassion. If the purpose were compassion, then even raising the skull could be justified, human or non-human or falsified out of plaster. Raise the skull with any other motive, and it becomes a sin.

He has turned from the crowd when two of the orphans find him. It is the first time they touch his hand.

'We found a medical tent, doctor sahib.'

'There's an Angrezi doctor there, and two nurses.'

'I need to see them,' says Masud.

Rimzim leads the way, a few steps ahead, chest out like a body-guard. Lucky holds Masud's hand.

'Where are the others?' asks Masud.

'Around,' says Lucky. 'Are you going to build a hospital here?'

'I don't know if I can do that.'

'We can't go back to your old hospital, right? It isn't safe for us there. You will have to build one here, in Pakistan.'

'This madness will end soon, boys. We will all go back home.'

Rimzim looks over his shoulder. 'But if you go back, doctor sahib, won't you have to treat everyone?'

'Yes. I would.'

'*Everyone?*'

'Remember yesterday, when you said you wanted to be a doctor?'

'I remember.'

'That is what doctors do.'

'I don't want to be a doctor, then,' Rimzim says, and waves his hand to dismiss the idea.

Lucky tugs Masud's hand. 'India has all the hospitals. Pakistan needs hospitals, right? Me and the other boys were thinking, we could help you build one. We could work there. We wouldn't take a salary, at first. But we would build a separate quarters where we would sleep and live.'

'I'm not working there if we're letting Hindus come,' insists Rimzim.

'We'll build it in Pakistan. This side of the border.' Lucky looks up at Masud. 'I can draw you the plans, if you like. I have them in my head.'

'I'd like to see them, Lucky.'

They have brought him to the six large, military-style tents that serve as the centre of the camp. A jeep is parked nearby, but it's uncertain how it got there, as no road seems to lead up to it. People, some seated, some standing, wait in long lines that wrap around the tent corners and intersect and lose coherence, merging with the formless crowds of the camp itself. Lucky kneels and traces a large rectangle in the dirt. Rimzim, for all his declarations, kneels too, interested in the blueprint the other boys have come up with and intending to make corrections to it. He also intends to keep the crowds from treading on their work. 'We'll have it ready when you come back,' Lucky promises.

Masud nods and approaches the red cross over the main tent. He is gazing out at the line when an English doctor in a pink-flecked white apron shoulders through the flap. He is towelling his hands and forearms, and he stops short on seeing Masud's black bag and European-style clothes, however filthy.

'Hello there,' he says. Masud turns. 'We weren't expecting a volunteer. Dr Alan Rutherford.'

Masud wipes his dirty right hand on his dirtier trouser leg and shakes the hand offered him. He is reminded of his medical student days, his professors, the contemptuous eye-rolling of his British classmates whenever he presented cases. The stammer, which had eased around the orphans, pinches his tongue and won't let go. He remembers the cards in his black bag. Rutherford takes one.

' "Dr Ibrahim Masud," ' he reads, the last syllable dwelled on for an extra second. ' "Paediatrics. Royal College." Class of '31, myself. We don't have a paediatrician here in the camp. Heaven knows we could use one. But if you need to rest beforehand . . . Have you come from far?'

'Out th-there,' says Masud, pointing.

'Have you worked at any of the other camps yet?'

'Out there,' Masud repeats. He raises his bag. 'I . . . I work.'

Rutherford shades his eyes. 'Out there? Do you mean the refugee columns?'

Masud nods.

'That's . . . that's incredibly brave of you, Dr Masud, but . . . but there's no need to have taken such a risk. If you wish to help, I can set you up here. There's plenty of work. We're getting more supplies driven down from Lahore this afternoon.'

Masud nods again. Rutherford eyes him. He wonders if Masud has been roughed up somehow while out caring for people in the column. Every one of his patients has stories of snatchings and stabbings, and not just at night. Rutherford is a selfless man, well into his second decade in India, for six of those years field surgeon to a Gurkha regiment; but for all his skill shooting a pistol on a range, and a build suited to the army, he is terrified to venture upstream into the kafila. Not without an armed escort, a convoy preferably, men in uniform with rifles over their shoulders. Enough bang and whizz to scatter the mobs. Selfless though his actions are, in his heart the barrier has not yet come down. He isn't part of the crowd he treats. He perceives himself as the refugees perceive him: the white British doctor, six foot four, tall enough to see the top of every head in his vicinity. Here to help. Here to suture and dress the crude things these people have done to each other with their daggers and scythes. His compassion is genuine, but so is his remove. His concern for Masud is genuine, too, when he says, 'You're welcome to rest until then.'

Masud nods as Rutherford waves in his next patient and re-enters the tent. I can see the restlessness that underlies Masud's stare. *These are the people who made it across*, he is thinking. *These are the ones who have already survived. The ones out* there, *though . . .*

Part of me stays beside Masud and keeps watch, but I have gone from the wind at his ear to a whisper.

First I whisk north, then north-west. Villages pass under me. The occasional column of smoke dimples inwards, and the swirls take on the shapes of my thoughts. I make out two boys holding each other: Shankar and Keshav, in a gravel ditch beside the train tracks. I see how Keshav slept, cheek on Shankar's shoulder, while Shankar shifted endlessly, forcing his panicked eyes shut but getting at best five or ten minutes' rest at a time. He spent the whole night in this slow suffocation. The image spreads into formless smoke.

I keep going. At a certain altitude I can sense the earth curve in every direction away from me. During my early wanderings, in those weeks right after I left my feverish cot, I feared I would leave the earth entirely, its gravity not strong enough to hold me in orbit. I feared I would be flung into the darkness that hides behind the brightest daylight. The sky, I realized, was just a partition between the world and an emptiness, an illusion put there to let us go about our work. The blue sky all this time no better than a painted ceiling. I felt the urge, too, to seep out of myself, dilute to nothing, my consciousness a colourless, odourless gas, undetectable.

I don't feel that now, though. I have never been so alive to the world, not even when I lived; never so close to the world, not even when I was in it. So I can go this high and dive at will, this time to Ayub's truck rattling down a country road, a quarter-mile from the kafila it tracks. I sit on the cabin and look down. Simran sits close to Aisha, wrists and ankles bound. She doesn't know her as Aisha, of course. To Simran, she is Kusum, stolen from her family in Sheikupura five days ago. For a time during the night, Simran had her cheek on Aisha's shoulder, the same way Keshav did on Shankar's. Only Aisha, too, was sleeping. When she woke up and saw Simran there, she moved her shoulder away, not wanting this intimacy, not wanting the responsibility that came with having protected her. The face with its small, girl features dropped and caught itself. Simran's eyes struggled open, drugged as though with opium, and she didn't seem to understand the rejection. Only after two straight hours of soft crying had she been able to sleep at all. She stayed awake until dawn and past dawn, terrified just by the proximity of Ayub sprawled lengthwise at the far end of the flatbed.

Qasim and Saif had smirked at him when he parked the truck and told them he was going in the back to sleep. He actually paused to speak as he pocketed the keys. 'Why are you smiling?'

'Save a little for us,' said Qasim.

'I'm going back there,' Ayub shot back, 'to protect my *investment.*' He used the English word. To his ear, the word made him sound shrewd, self-possessed, cold—above the itch and small heat that agitated men like Qasim and Saif.

Aisha had sensed that in him perfectly, knowing men as well as she did. Muslim, Hindu, Sikh, she had seen them all, and they were more alike than they thought. She knew how the feeling of power made the sensation of pleasure possible for them. So when she saw Ayub raising Simran off the ground, and the other two approaching, the skinny one biting his thumbnail in uneasy fascination, she knew what to say to Ayub. Two sentences, almost a riddle, in brusque, brash, village-girl Urdu. 'Don't let them bite the apple you mean to sell, Ayub mian. No one's *that* hungry.'

Don't let them: She implied he was the calculating leader who had to keep the wild other ones in check. By denying Saif and

Qasim—and himself—Ayub would exert more power than by forcing Simran. Referring to Simran as an item to be sold made him realize how much more this piece would sell for, intact. None of this was communicated directly. A push from Aisha would have made him push back. Immediately after her comment, she yawned and withdrew—a show of indifference so he wouldn't think she was trying to work her own will.

Ayub looked at Aisha and then back at Simran, still not lowering her. One of Simran's hands shot up to the roots of her hair and back over her chest again, unable to decide on the greater emergency. The pain, or the shame.

Qasim adjusted himself with a finger and spat to the side. 'I'm second.'

Ayub glanced his way in irritation.

Saif made it worse, hand digging in his kameez pocket. 'I have a coin.'

Ayub turned to Saif and gave a loud shush. Saif's hand stopped moving, slunk out of the pocket, and hung at his side. Ayub dropped Simran, and her legs buckled as she landed. He shook her clothes one more time to be sure, then threw them on her bowed head of hair. 'Get dressed.'

She got back into her clothes while they watched. Ayub noticed the smell of the exhaust just then and glanced angrily at Qasim. 'Why haven't you turned off the engine yet? It's a waste of fuel.'

It had been Ayub, of course, who left it running in the first place. Qasim knew better than to point that out. Ayub pointed to the bed of the truck and told Simran, 'Climb on.' She didn't move but kept glancing at Aisha, who had laid back on her bedding and faced the night sky. A twist of Simran's ear brought her to her feet, her body wincing towards his hand.

Ayub followed her on to the truck. Staring up at him, she scrambled away on her heels and hands until her back hit a hard surface. She found herself beside Aisha, on one end of her bedding, the stains on it stiff, rough as scabs. But he came after her only to bind her wrists and ankles. He tied her tighter than he had the other two. When his loops and figure eights were finished, he ran his hand up her soft inner forearm, just once. An indulgence. Aisha saw it and knew what it meant: the girl might last this night out, but not the next.

The blueprint has grown in the dust by the time Masud returns. Small squares crowd inside a spacious rectangle. Children Masud has never seen before, children of the camp, have come to watch. 'We're building a hospital,' Lucky explains to the crowd. Masud arrives during the tour Lucky gives the other children. A stick points to the rooms and wings. 'This is where the sick people wait. In this room, right next to it, me, Billi and Rimzim take the patient in and do a full check-up, complete, everything. Our doctor sahib sits here, in the examining room, and we go in and tell him how this next person has a problem with his heart, this next person has a problem keeping his food down, that kind of thing. Then he says, all right, I have to operate. So this room here is where he does his operations.

Big operations, the kind they can't even do in London, that's what he does here. At night, after we clean up, this is where the assistants eat and sleep. It's our living quarters. It's going to have a kitchen, a kabaddi ground, a schoolhouse, everything . . .'

Afterwards, Masud joins the end of the line outside the medical tent. Children come and go. The coin of his stethoscope bell set on each chest, they listen to their own hearts. The day is so hot he doesn't have to rub it warm against his palm.

The sight of the children delighting in the instrument reminds me of Shankar and Keshav playing, in my last days, with my own black bag, my own stethoscope. I had no use for the instruments by then. The twins weren't old enough to understand, but I sat up one afternoon, brought their faces side by side, put one earpiece in Keshav's left ear, one in Shankar's right, and had them listen to my heart. I held my breath so they wouldn't hear my wet wheeze. They weren't at an age when they sat still very long, and soon they were both grabbing for the bell. Keshav grabbed the cord and made off with the stethoscope entirely, and Shankar wailed until Sonia picked him up. Keshav also loved putting the bulb of my blood pressure monitor in his mouth. I always kept an eye on the pressure column because I was afraid it would snap and spill the poisonous mercury. That was only one of the hundreds of things I worried about on that helpless cot. I wish I had let up worrying and just rejoiced in watching them play. Even the screaming matches had something sweet in them, if only I had been receptive. But I was impatient with life and death alike. There were whole days I longed for silence. There were whole nights I longed for clamour.

Two hours later, Dr Rutherford looks up and sees Masud walked in by a nurse. He recognizes him and stands up to shake his hand, but Masud points down and says, 'Foot.' He begins to undo his shoelaces.

'Good God, man, I had no idea you came as a patient. I would have taken you right away. Please. Here. Is this the foot, then?'

He guides Masud to the examining table and cups his shoe heel. The dust of the road flakes off on his bare palm. I had forgotten about it, too, but there it is, that first careless razor cut Masud suffered outside his house. His mind has refused to acknowledge it until now. I didn't even see him limp. If I think back, though, I should have seen the way he shifted his weight to the other foot whenever he wasn't walking. The lame dog in his escort always got thrown the largest scrap of roti, tail high and swinging, slack paw held gingerly off the ground.

The cut's splayed edges have turned a dusky bluish-black. Beyond this, the whole back of his foot glows pink, almost to the shin. It looks like something he might have treated on the road. Medically, I am shocked any infection could have progressed this far in only forty-eight hours, even accounting for the damp, hot shoe. It's as if his cut stained itself this colour by leeching some trace of infection from every wound he treated.

Rutherford scoots back on his wheeled stool, partly from the shock of the cut, partly from the smell. 'This is going to need an aggressive debridement,' he shakes his head. 'Fresh dressings, changed twice daily. Penicillin would work wonders. Our field hospitals had it when I served in France. Splendid drug. But there's no getting any out here.'

Masud looks down. Out of his bag he takes the empty iodine bottle and the lone shred of gauze.

'Oh, certainly—disinfectant. I can get you disinfectant. We can clean and dress it for now. Nasty wound there . . . some of this tissue may well have to be cut out. I'll get you seen first thing. Our surgeon should be here soon. He was scheduled to be here already, of course, but circumstances held him up where he was, I imagine. Roads can't be smooth going between here and Rawalpindi.'

Masud nods as Rutherford gestures his nurse over, and they set to work. It gives me great satisfaction to see Masud's foot being washed, and by an Englishman at that—that's always what humble kings are doing to wise Brahmins, in our stories. They always have a basin brought and wash the dust off the wandering holy man's lotus-pink feet.

It means even more to me because I know Masud is not finished walking.

I can almost always get a clear read on people. Each mind swims in its skull before me like a fish in a glass bowl. But with Aisha right now—the truck parked again, Saif told to stay back and watch the girls—I can't see clearly how she feels about Simran. The water is murky, the glass frosted.

Saif is easier to read. He doesn't want the girls to know he is lowest ranked among the three, that Ayub doesn't trust him on the hunt. He wants to project power, command, aggression. So he paces back and forth, trying to keep up a show of masculine energy, fists at his sides. Periodically he checks up the road as if there were some specific threat he were stationed here to watch for. He wants to impress them. Simran in particular. The strutting doesn't last very long. He goes around the side of the truck. They can hear the patter of his urine in the dust. After that, some more strutting. At last he tires of it, squats in the sun, and stares straight ahead. He spits to the side on occasion, waves away a fly if it lands on his ear or lip.

Simran I can read, too. Naturally she feels close to Aisha. She is not certain what Aisha said the previous night; she was too scared to understand the words said to her or around her. Her refusal to follow Ayub's commands had not been defiance, just the slack limbs of prey in the jaw. Whatever Aisha said, it had called off the men. Simran had got her clothes back. Though by then, of course, it was too late. They had all seen her. I see the intense shame that surges and subsides in her like nausea. She cannot bear to look at Saif, or even to let Saif see her face. The whole time he guards the truck, she keeps her face between her knees and packs herself as deeply into a corner as she can. Uma blocks his view of her from some angles, but not from all. This is how bad she feels from being *seen*. If she were to be touched . . .

It's part of what confuses Aisha's feelings towards Simran: Her vulnerability, her hypersensitivity to things Aisha herself scarcely registers. Like the gaze of men. When she first alerted Ayub to Simran walking up the road, she had assumed the girl was detritus, like Uma. Her mouth had gone dry with guilt to see terrified innocence. It wasn't the thing she had intended to deliver. So she intervened.

PARTITIONS

As soon as the truck ground to life under them and Simran fell weeping on her shoulder, Aisha regretted delaying the violence. Hard thoughts chipped at her guilt. How long would Simran have lasted out there before some gang cut her up? Better to be merchandise; she would be kept in good condition if someone spent money to acquire her, and even better condition if she earned an income, as Aisha did. Still, the guilt hasn't gone away, and neither has the sense of ownership. *Two bangs with my fist on that cabin window*, Aisha thinks, *have altered this child's life, permanently.*

At least that is what I *think* I read in her—but I see, simultaneously, a second, wholly separate set of thoughts. It's the split that allows her to surrender her body three or four times on an average night. It works at every level. So the first mind thinks about guilt and regret. The second mind realizes she can exploit this trust, tell Simran the stories that will keep her docile, a willing captive. Isn't that what she has been paid to do? She has an obligation, doesn't she? Besides, it is merciful to tell Simran these lies. The lies will reconcile her to her captivity, make her believe things will be harder off the truck than on it.

So Aisha went to work on her in the morning and by now, with a few spells of rest, has told her the stories she has heard and some she has invented. How families don't take back daughters who have been in captivity. How villages hold such girls lower than dogs, lower even than their untouchables. The story about the friend of hers they burned alive. Stories about the gangs out in the countryside—if a girl didn't have protectors, like Ayub bhaiyya, they would gag her in a cave and keep her there for a week, a public woman. This truck was taking them to Lahore, where the men would find them work, place them in good households.

Aisha did her job as the Scheherazade, facts and lies mated into stories, until Simran looked at her and responded with her own account, in three sentences, of how she came here. The bloodstain on her front and the bloodstain on her back. Aisha went quiet after that.

Simran went on to dream aloud about Amritsar and service in the temple there. At that moment, the partition between Aisha's first and second mind, the woman's and the whore's, tore open. Waters divided until then mixed, and the mixture grew murky.

It's that murk I'm staring into when I try to read Aisha. But her confusion gives me hope. If there is one thing dangerously abundant right now, it is certainty. Certainty makes possible in men the most extreme good and the most extreme evil. A land like the Punjab, five rivers and three faiths, could do with a little less certainty.

My thoughts switch back to Saif. I am startled by the new geyser of happiness inside him. Ayub and Qasim are slogging back to the van. Ayub has brought back scratches, Qasim, a new limp. Whatever they attempted without Saif's help has gone awry, it seems. Qasim, waving Saif away, claims he stepped across a ditch wrong, and Ayub doesn't contradict him, letting him save face. The nail marks across Ayub's cheek have their own story, but he doesn't care enough about Saif's opinion to come up with a falsehood. Saif rejoices to see them empty-handed, even though it means less money for him as well.

I know better than to rejoice for whatever girl they failed to bring in. The fact that she is not here doesn't mean she escaped. Ayub and Qasim aren't in a hurry. Their minds are curiously blank of any memory of what has just happened, or at least of any memory I can access. I suspect that she fought hard, and that they fought back harder—knowing Ayub, too hard. I scan half a kilometre, every direction. Sure enough, I find a girl's body tucked into a gulch. She's the one, I suspect. The berry that ruptured bright and red between their fingers.

The surgeon arrives a little over an hour after Masud's wound is dressed. The shoe feels tight now. It stays on in spite of the laces being more or less undone, tucked under the tongue so he won't tread on them. Swollen and split, the shoe mimics the cut it covers.

An open jeep and a truck squeeze and angle miraculously between the tents. Children jog beside the truck and dart close to tap its sides. They think it brings water and food. The surgeon, Dr Tahir, is a military man, a surgeon in the newly formed Pakistani Army. He grips the overhead bar and sways with the potholes. A thin scarf keeps the road dust from his nose and mouth, but the trade-off is heat. Sweat and hair oil slick his forehead. Dark ovals soak his back, chest and underarms. When he steps from the jeep, gratefully undoing the scarf to pat his forehead and temples, Rutherford and three other camp physicians come forward bearing lists of the most emergent cases. In spite of what Rutherford said earlier, Masud's name is not on his list. Masud wouldn't have wanted that anyway. Trimming the dead skin off his careless razor-nick mustn't delay the amputation of feet gone outright gangrenous.

No greetings are exchanged besides a meeting of eyes and a brief nod. Tahir listens expressionlessly to the cases waiting for him. Grease blackens his fingers, and he raises his hands. It looks to me, at first, like namaaz, but really it's the pose surgeons take after they have scrubbed, hands immaculate and elbows dripping. A nurse understands. There is no running water in the camp, so she brings a bottle of sterile saline and pours once to wet his hands and forearms. He scrubs thoroughly. When his thumb and fore-finger make a ring and milk the filth down his arm, the suds gather at his wrists, a black cuff. Another rinse, another round of soap. Finally the rest of the water pours into the dirt. He slides his hands and arms under the tilted bottle. Rutherford glances uneasily at the refugees, who have gathered to watch the new arrival. To their thirst, it is drinking water. But they have seen too much to be out-raged. They can believe anything of reality.

Rutherford looks past the soldiers unloading the supply truck into the medical tents. So he doesn't see Masud helping them. At first the soldiers are wary handing boxes to this thin, elderly man. He looks like just one more wastrel refugee who happens to be sheathed in a gentleman's clothes. But he makes the trips with unusual vigour, sometimes two boxes stacked past his chin. Then, at one point, he stops coming. They never wonder what has become of him.

I can see him. His body is tilted, his arm flexed a few degrees, tendons taut at the crook of the elbow to carry his black bag. It is much heavier now, stuffed until it can't close, like his shoe. I see six bottles of iodine, sterilely packaged scalpels, scissors, needles, syringes. His waistband is padded with gauze packages, the belt buckled two holes wider. He is sneaking away before the children, still gathered around the truck and jeep, can notice his departure and follow. Where he is going, it won't be safe for them. Or for him. The dogs, though, are everywhere at the same risk, everywhere just as safe. They catch wind of his passage, turn to his diminishing figure, and hurry off to join him.

Shankar and Keshav have no bodyguards. On crowded open-air platforms or unpeopled tracks, they walk alone. Inquiries are no use, nor is Keshav's description of his mother, arm up and on tiptoe to communicate her height. So many people everywhere, but no one has seen anyone. The twins watch for longer periods at each station, but not because their hope is strengthening. Shankar needs the breaks. Mouth open, neck veins starting to swell, he watches. The crowds slosh and stir against the invisible dam of the platform edge, the station filling like a reservoir, people flowing in from miles around. A train arrives, and they surge into its leaks and holes. The train passes on. The boys stare hardest then, eyes eager for whatever new reality the rear edge of the train unveils. Usually only a few puddles of people and baggage remain. Or else it's just new strangers switched in for the old strangers.

All this time their eyes are open, and I can't stop the world from pouring in. I think of their eyes as open wounds I want to keep clean. If I can keep them clean, I can keep them from getting infected, and then those wounds won't weep. When they hear violence coming, when they hear the drums, the gleeful wolf whistles, the rare pistol-shot (most of the killing happens intimately, blade or bludgeon), they hide. In ravines, in fields of wheat or sugarcane. Behind stray uncoupled cars if they are near a station. Shankar closes his mouth and breathes as best he can through his nose, desperate to mute his gasping and labouring. I stand between them and what they see, but the meshwork of me is all too fine.

A thin old man I could have mistaken for Masud, both from his shape and his trousers and shirt, is stopped by a dozen boys. He is a Muslim, and so are these boys. Hands joined, he calls them his sons, his protectors. They demand to know his name. 'You know me, boys. I am your teacher, Mr Shah.' *Your full name, sisterfucker,* one of the boys shouts. Another boy shoves him. He scoots back a step but stays on his feet, keeps his hands joined. 'Ahmed Shah, Ahmed Shah.' *Amit is a Hindu name, sisterfucker.* 'Ahmed. You know me. Ahmed.' *So is Shah. Are you lying to us, Amit?* 'Ahmed Shah. Ahmed Shah.' *We'll see if you're one of us. We'll see if you pass the test.* Laughing aloud, they pull at his belt and drop his trousers. My twins can see the slack skin of the old schoolteacher's buttocks, each knee like the raw knob in a bole swollen by a parasite, his dignity puddled around his ankles; and, facing them, the mocking faces of the students, lit by their torches. *You pass, old man! But just barely!* One boy snatches his spectacles, searches deep and spits into each lens, then sets the glasses back on the old man's face, dripping viscous. The papers that have fallen from the teacher's satchel catch on a rare breeze. I see an equilateral triangle on one sheet, a dashed line down the middle of it. Bisection. I see Arabic numerals and the Hindu zero and Europe's decimal point giving each other magnitude and place. Keshav breaks cover and gathers the papers. I snatch in vain at his shirt; Shankar's weak arm shadows my movement exactly, but we both miss. He is lucky their laughter throws back their heads and shuts their eyes as they pass on.

Once they are around the corner, the old man feels safe to move again. He buckles his belt. He wipes his glasses on an untucked shirt tail, reclaims them with his own spit, and wipes them again. Keshav runs to him with the gathered papers, and the teacher's small, raw eyes see only a small figure running his way. It's enough to scare him, and he skips a step back. His glasses tremble back on to his nose, askew, and he accepts the gift. Shankar and I want to scold Keshav for that dangerous kindness, but neither of us have the breath to do it.

Masud looks for a kafila's passage like the one vein of ore in a mine. The distances feel longer here, the night more haunted. When he left the camp, the luck that guided him there deserted him, as though seeking out risk like this were ingratitude. Even with his lean, scarred bodyguards, he feels on his own. They sense his new vulnerability, too, and cluster closer than he remembers. Sometimes they slant so sharply across his path, he wonders whether they mean to pass between his legs. The second time he stops and says, 'Now, friends, did you see how I almost tripped that time? What will you do if this old man falls and breaks a hip?' There's more ease in his tone of voice than in his mind. He hasn't felt this way since dusk in the city. The same changes are overcoming him, the dry mouth that doesn't mean thirst, the sweat that isn't the heat's fault. But he keeps walking.

When he finds them, he wonders if he wandered in a circle and ended up joining the same kafila that bore him to Pakistan. The faces here resemble the faces there. The clothes are the same, the bundles and mules and families the same. Gashes often run at the same angles. The relationship of attacker to victim flash before him, plain as statuary: this gash glanced across the shoulder of someone running away; this one struck the forearm of someone who saw the blade descending and tried to block it. Everything is familiar. It's only after he gets close that he can see the residual flecks of bindis on the Hindu women, or the steel kangans and hard topknots on the devout Sikhs. Externals, indistinct in the twilight, unseen by nightfall—yet precisely at nightfall, the marks by which they are targeted.

They look up and see him coated in ash, surrounded by subservient animals. Were it not for the black bag and trouser legs, they would have thought him an ascetic. One elderly woman, delirious, murmurs a strange word at the sight of him: 'Pashupati.' The rest of her talk concerns events of the prior century and shouts against imaginary assailants, and I am the only one to catch the word. It means 'Father of the Animals'. It's a name for Shiva. So is Shankar.

There have always been stories, of course, and even the stories are the same—only this time they say what the Muslims did to them, to their families and homes and farms. Masud does his work and listens. He is not here to fight their hatred. He is here to fight their suffering. That is all. So he clicks shut a haemostat on his crescent-shaped suture needle and bends to his work while a father or brother weeps and swears vengeance on all Islam. It is only once, after he has set and slung a child's arm by moonlight, that a mother asks to know the doctor's name. Her husband and she have just told him a story, too, how the Mussulmaans stomped the boy's arm against a stair when he wouldn't reveal where the rest of the family had gone to hide. He had looked at the boy and said, 'Brave, very brave.'

And now, opening three tins of food before him, she wants to know his name. It would be easy to lie. Hindu names and Sikh names come to mind. Instead he joins his hands and tells the truth, without a stammer, with no title to distract from it. 'Ibrahim Allama Masud.'

The girl they took the first day, the younger of the two sisters, is dead, more or less. Aisha complains the girl hasn't stirred all day. Ayub waits for a stretch of empty road before he pulls over and rolls her. He can tell something is wrong by the way the shoulders lift but the rest lies flat. It takes a hand on her shoulder and another on her hip to get her on to her back. He carried her before, and he can compare. She was lighter before. A few slaps awaken nothing. That is the only way he knows to check for life. Her face is flat where she laid on it, while the rest of it is puffy, the haemorrhage having pooled black around her eye sockets. Finally Ayub scoops her in both arms, like a sleeping daughter. He gets off the truck and lays her body on the ground. This time, when it is too late, he handles her with great care, almost tenderness—setting her buttocks down first, then lowering, by degrees, her back, her skull. At the end, he eases her head up with his left hand and slides his right hand free. He spits to the side, clips a bidi between his lips, and strikes a match.

Saif and Qasim are staring at Ayub. Qasim is wondering whether Ayub will show rage at last—two botched abductions on what was supposed to be their last day, and now the first piece turns out to have been damaged, unusable. Saif actually feels triumphant. His humiliation the first day, in his struggle with the older sister, has been redeemed. *I bet he wishes he'd kept mine*, Saif thinks. *Bringing mine in, all I broke was her tooth. Not her skull.* But he is wary of saying this out loud, no matter how much he wants the truth acknowledged. Maybe he will breach it to Qasim later. When Ayub goes in the back to sleep—that's when Saif will point out how right he'd been, from the start, to finesse the sister down the exactly as he had. They should have learned from him.

I can see Saif's vanity swelling again. Every time he thinks about himself (and that is often), he gets restless, I notice. One extreme or the other. One moment, he believes the others are laughing over him. The next moment, he dreams himself the descendant of conquerors. Right now, in his own estimation, he is shrewder, stronger, set apart. His posture has straightened a little to match.

Ayub has become conscious of the others looking at him. His thoughts until now have been exclusively of money. During his long stare at the girl, he was manipulating pitiless numbers in his head. They are watching. 'One raid tonight, while we're close to the border. Then we're heading back west to Lahore in the morning,' he says. 'If nothing else, we'll sell the two we have.'

Neither Saif nor Qasim say anything. Simran, on the truck, glances at Uma, then whispers to Aisha, 'Two? But there are three of us.'

Aisha looks down and says nothing. If it weren't so dark, I could have seen her flush. This, too, gives me hope.

Ayub stubs the bidi in the unconscious girl's navel, crushing it in deep. An umbilical braid of white smoke grows out of her. He walks between Qasim and Saif, and they part for him, as he intends them to. Ayub is pleased with his gesture, stubbing the bidi like that and striding between them . . . he dwells on it for a part of the drive, how cold and hard and in-command he must have appeared to everyone. But the feeling wears off, and he goes back to brooding on the four hundred rupees he has left on the roadside.

They aren't on the road long before Qasim, in the passenger seat, eyes hooded sensuously in the loud night wind, points at the rear-view mirror and shouts. The sweep of a choli, and heels in the truck's tail lights as white as spots on a hind. Simran timed her jump to Ayub's slowing-down before the larger holes in the road—it's his cousin's truck, and he had been going gently over the shocks. She landed without spraining anything and started running. If she had just ran straight for the sugarcane field, Qasim wouldn't have seen her. The instinct to run the other way crossed with the desire to hide herself in the field. So she ended up running a diagonal.

Her appearance in the mirror, which lasted only four or five seconds, synchronized exactly with the pothole's jarring Qasim's eyes open. It's on a dot of time this small that Simran's life is going to pivot.

Ayub brakes hard. The cabin lurches, and Qasim locks both arms stiff on the dash. Saif hurls forward and slams his flank. He squirms across Qasim's startled chest. The cloud of dust that scrapes up around the truck has the pallor of moon dust. I raise the palms of my hands through it and briefly see my familiar long fingers, down to the prophetic lines. The suggestion shatters as Saif bursts through the dust and through me.

He has thrust himself through the passenger window, feet first, and is already running as Ayub opens the door. Simran finally turns into the sugarcane field and vanishes. I see the place she goes in. Saif is close enough to see it, too, and plunges through the same swish. Qasim, also running, shouts at Saif to *run after her, run, run,* but he stops at the spot where Saif entered the field. There is something about the field's darkness and size that scares me, too, as if these vast, shivering rustles were hundreds of brooms effacing me. Qasim shouts one more time, chest heaving.

'What happened?' Ayub snaps.

Aisha dangles a length of limp rope and tosses it towards him. 'Which one of you tied her up?' Ayub snatches the rope, wraps his hands with it, and pulls it taut. His body shakes with the frustration, or else with the tension of so many opposing muscles firing at once. '*Take her down, Saif!*' he bellows at the field. Uma stirs and cowers lower behind her propped-up knees.

Saif is swatting aside the ticklish stalks. He hears his name in the distance and runs harder, but it is still slow-going. He goes fastest when his eyes are closed. Simran knows he is after her and has started sobbing as she runs. This is another mistake. Sound is the only way he can target her. He struggles to keep track of her sobbing over the stalks he shakes and the huff of his own panting. She runs with one arm over her downturned face, one hand groping forward, like a woman with acid splashed in her eyes. When his hand smacks her back, the impact feels hollow to him. The hooped barrel of her ribs, empty. She stumbles, both arms out, balance lost. Her body falls in the direction it was just running; the movement is out of her control now. He slams blindly into her, chest to back. It tips her forward. He falls, too, landing beyond her, only part of her under him, what seems to be her head under his leg. But the rest of her is free, and she bats his leg aside and scampers back. He lunges. The sugarcane stalks shake and shed. She is still getting away, her kicks startlingly strong. His head snaps away from her, his eyes flinch shut, and his shoulders shrug protectively, defending himself even as he grabs for her. A sudden panic comes over him—what kind of man does it make him, if he can't even subdue this slight girl? Would another man, would Ayub or Qasim, have this much trouble? He snarls aloud, to exhort himself, to make himself feel powerful and savage, and doing so he makes another full-body lunge.

She is at once softer and harder than the pillows his bachelor-hood has rutted on all these years. His first excitement isn't even sexual. He has been a scavenger his whole life. For the first time he has actually run something down, and that is what excites him. Chased it and outrun it and taken it down. One kind of excitement feeds the next. Where are the others? The others are never going to find them this deep in the field. He was running for minutes, min-utes—tracing her by sound, his senses aroused, like a real predator. They are all alone here. Only the moonlight penetrates. Quiet. His panting. The tussle of her body against the sun-bleached leaf chaff on the ground—which is also the rolling and straining of her body against his. He wonders briefly if she might be feeling lust right now, under a man's weight for the first time. A body-wide reflex, maybe, surprising her. A cracking and loosening, a flow, maybe, that takes place against her will. What did her *body* know of fear or revulsion? Her body must want things, he thinks, her mind doesn't allow. It is like that with all girls. So he wants to know. What are the consequences, here, in the middle of a sugarcane field, at night? Strangely enough, it's curiosity that tugs at her drawstring and snakes his fingers between her legs. At this point, at the start of this, he doesn't intend to damage the piece. Though he has fantasized often enough by now about breaking the seal, sometimes thought about it in the humming truck itself, between Ayub and Qasim, his forearms crossed to conceal his stub erection. He still thinks of Simran as money. He just wants to feel, to know, to be the first man ever to touch her there. And to see if something might take over in her body and make her seek more of the sensation. After all, he thinks, there is nothing stopping him, he's hidden on all sides. She's hardly going to go and complain to Ayub.

He feels. Damp but not wet. The mouth pursed. He had not expected so much coarse hair. She is older than he first thought. Her nails sink in his forehead and scratch down. He squinches his eyes and bucks back. His hand stays where it is; his free hand grabs one wrist and then the other and forces them to the ground. Now that she's secured there, arms lusciously overhead, like a nautch girl pantomiming a snake, he slides off to kneel beside her. Blood trails down his nose and drips on her face. Doesn't she know how he can punish her? Doesn't she respect him? She doesn't respect him. She has seen him humiliated in front of the others. How dare she not fear him? How dare she still struggle? How dare she not plead for mercy? He scrubs at her with the flat of his hand, hard, as if he were rubbing a stain out of wool. Her legs kick wildly at first but then contract to her chest as the pain strikes her silent. He throws his head down and bites the soft flesh of the bosom where he has seen bite marks on Uma. It is as satisfying as meat. He wishes he could tear off and chew what he has gathered between his teeth. His hand jerks free and out and covers his mouth and nose. He breathes. The scent, at once new and familiar, dizzies him. His clamp on her wrists weakens with it. He must not let this chance go. His eyes close. He is never going to get anything this lovely and young and clean, ever. He is going to go through the rest of his life and never get anything this good. A sudden, biological desperation surges through him. *This is my only chance to have a girl like this.*

Her hands have slipped free. She rolls and is on her feet again before his eyes can open, running, one hand clutching her undone drawstring, the other over the depressions of his teeth, ripening blood-vivid in the moonlight, like pomegranate seeds. He follows and breaks through the edge of the sugarcane field on to an unexpected road.

His quarry crouches bawling behind a tall, bony old man dressed in an Englishman's tatters. He is bent slightly at the waist, turned away from Saif. He holds his palm flat over Simran, as if he wished to stroke her crying, but has hesitated. As if he were blessing her. Around them, a phalanx of dogs locks into place, assesses Saif with scowls and faint whistles, and starts up a frenzied barking.

Masud sees the wiry figure against the sugarcane. The man's shoulders heave, and he holds his arms at a distance from his sides. It's the blood on his face and forehead that makes Masud wonder if Saif and Simran are a couple, pursued together through the field by some third assailant, or a gang of assailants. So he shushes the dogs once, and they go quiet one by one, reluctantly.

Masud turns up his palm and moves it side to side, asking the question, *What?*

'She's mine,' says Saif, pointing. His mind, rapid with adrenaline, assesses the old man as weak and possibly a deaf-mute. But the dogs seem keenly trained to his commands. Saif can't advance. He has to intimidate. 'If you don't give her up, I'll bring my friends and find you. You, your dogs, the girl, no one will get away.'

Simran whispers through a throat hoarse with shrieking. 'Don't give me up. They're going to sell me. Please don't give me up. *Please*. Your God will bless you. Please.'

Masud shakes his head, scarcely comprehending. Tears blur his eyes as the idea of it comes home. He sees where Simran is holding herself and his face crushes into a grimace. He had deadened himself, as every physician deadens himself, to what the wounds on the refugee women implied; he had not thought about it, never imagined it. Otherwise how could he have ever moved on to the next patient? But here it is at last, the violence in progress, as it is happening. The dozens of female bodies he has treated, each one an aftermath, shake his memory. He tries to speak. 'S-s-sell?'

'It's our business, old man. If not us, someone else. Give her here.'

Masud reaches in his pocket and takes out the fat wallet he saved from his burning house. He steps between the dogs, drops it in the dirt, and retreats. His hands join.

Saif stares in awe at the money. There are enough notes there ... he can skim *hundreds* and present the remainder as her purchase price. He smiles. His attention is off Simran. He comes forward and reaches down. He isn't even thinking about the dogs.

He should be. As soon as he touches the money, Masud's invisible hold on them breaks. All seven launch at Saif noiselessly. Right fist still clutching the money, but his arms and flanks dangling spry, bony dogs, Saif staggers howling into the sugarcane.

As soon as that howling stops—and it stops as soon as Saif's throat is low enough to the ground—the whistle of a train replaces it. Masud's arm covers Simran, who cries harder now that she feels safe. She cries so hard she coughs, coughs so hard she vomits. Not food. Only the dark green bile of an empty stomach. Masud stays beside her. He looks up at the sound of the eastbound train, and his ears twitch back like an alert animal's. I see him thinking how those tracks could lead them into India, where this girl will be safer. Provided he can get her to a camp there. The whistle stops, replaced by a distant clacking. The tracks are straight ahead.

The border isn't far. Masud, though wandering upstream in the kafila, has drifted farther east in its current than he knows. Ayub was bringing the truck closer to the border, hoping to catch this kafila at its fullest, after every tributary in the countryside had flowed into it.

Keshav and Shankar aren't far, either. They are just past the border, passing with the tracks through one of hundreds of small border villages that have sifted, by chance, to one side or another of the line. They have arrived, though they don't realize it, in India.

I leave Saif in the sugarcane field, Masud and Simran on the road. I disperse into the hot night and collect in front of my boys. I walk backwards, facing them. Keshav has his arm over Shankar the same way Masud has his over Simran. It can't be long now. Everything in medicine says it should have happened hours ago. For him to have lasted until now . . . It can't be long.

And it isn't long. I am with them only minutes when Shankar collapses. He drops face first, leaving empty the curve of Keshav's arm. When Keshav turns him on to his back, the first thing he sees is his brother's bleeding nose, and he uses his sleeve to dab at it. Shankar doesn't respond to his name. He doesn't respond to a shake of his arm, a hand on his cheek. In the moonlight, Keshav can see the veins on his brother's neck, huge, rounded, fluttering strangely. The biggest one gives a little under his fingertip. He comes back to Shankar's face, grips it in both hands, speaks to him. The head drops to one side when he lets go. That is when Keshav hears it.

Hare hare Mahadev!

Mahadev: like Shankar, another name for Shiva.

Hare hare Mahadev!

Sixteen Hindu men are burning the house of a Muslim lawyer. The lawyer fled across the border days ago. He left one hundred and eight thick leatherbound volumes of jurisprudence here, and one slimmer but infinite Qur'an. The bonfire has been set up in the courtyard. Some of the men are inside the gate, some are whistling outside, clapping flames into the sky like spooked birds.

Hare hare Mahadev!

'Those are our people, Shankar!' Keshav whispers excitedly. 'Those are Hindus! Did you hear? Those are Hindus!'

He has a vision of all these men following him to this spot and carrying Shankar to a police jeep or a bus and driving, fast, to some tall, clean hospital. He leaves his brother's side and breaks into a run. The burning house shines on his eyes, so lately wet with tears.

Jaggu, Bhupinder, Mangal, Indrajit, Amar, Apu, Hasmukh . . . I search their minds the way they searched the drawers in that burning house. They found no jewellery. I find no mercy. I know what kind of human beings these are. And Keshav is running towards them. It is a meaningless reflex, I know, but I scoop my arm across his stomach the way I used to when he was small and had just learned to walk and headed recklessly for the stairs. He doesn't even register it as a protesting wind.

Hare hare Mahadev!

The one named Jaggu grabs him by the collar. It's the kameez the widow Shanaaz put on him. Keshav is still explaining, pointing behind him to where Shankar lies unconscious. He doesn't understand what is happening. The others turn from the fire and smile at the child.

'What's your name, chhote mian?'

'Keshav!'

'What was that? Qasif?'

Keshav shakes his head, afraid to speak. The hold on his collar has tightened, and the cloth cuts into his neck. In the light from the house, I can see Jaggu's tobacco-ravaged teeth. His paan-pink, clown-lurid lips.

'Where did you come from, Qasif mian?'

Keshav knows something has gone wrong. These are his people, Hindus, he heard them chanting, he can see the tilaks on their foreheads. 'But we're the *same*,' he chokes. 'My brother—'

'Where did you come from?'

Keshav points.

'Hasmukh! Say, isn't that way Pakistan?'

Hasmukh, whose name means 'smiling face', keeps smiling. Amar, whose name means 'deathless', picks up one of the red metal fuel cans lined up along the outer wall of the lawyer's bungalow. While he unscrews the cap, Jaggu puts his thumb and forefinger to either side of Keshav's chin.

'Tell me, cute boy, is your home in Pakistan?'

Keshav nods. It is, after all. Or was.

'Then what are you doing in *Hindustan*? This isn't your country. You know that, right?'

The can bucks and sloshes.

'You know that, right?'

Jaggu lets go of Keshav's collar and steps away from the splash. Keshav is surrounded by these men now, and he stands trembling in the hot night while the paraffin soaks his hair, his clothes. Amar walks around him clockwise, thorough, making sure the back gets doused, too. The shirt drenches transparent and sticks to his small chest and stomach, rising and falling rapidly. Keshav's eyes look from man to man. Hindu to fellow Hindu.

Jaggu has brought a matchbox out of his pocket. His thumb slides the matchbox open. His middle finger slides it shut. He tilts the matchbox, striking surface up, the match in his other hand aslant, the dainty pinky lifted clear.

· Six ·

Settlements

I am nothing if not cold. I am nothing if not air. I am nothing, granted, but I am here.

I can see the match head in detail, the bulb of phosphorus-studded russet. The cross-hatched friction strip on the edge of the matchbox. The matchbox itself, printed with a playing card, Ace of Hearts. Every pit and white fleck in his fingernails. Three fingers, brought together the same way as when he brings a pinch of roti to his mouth. In those fingers, the pale stick. Descending casually, expertly. Jaggu has been striking them all night, striking them and dropping them and admiring each blaze like a sunrise.

No you don't. No. You. Don't.

Physics ordains that I cannot interfere. That these processes are stronger than I am. The passage of matter through space. A scratch unlocking a chemical flare. The slap of paraffin on the nape of a neck, the side of a face.

The can pauses high over Keshav's head to drip its last. Amar, Hindu brother, defender of the dharma, co-religionist, shakes a few last drops out and tosses it aside.

'Send him home, Jaggu.'

That is my boy.

I gather every bit of me into arms, legs, torso, head. My insubstantial presence grows denser and denser until I am, at last, a substantial absence. A body-shaped uptick in barometric pressure. An effigy of cold air, arm straight out, gripping that matchbox in its fist.

No you don't.

The match flares and goes out, all in the same motion. I still can't tell if it was my hand or the match itself. Jaggu holds up the smoking head and drops. A dud, he decides. He slides out another one. He has plenty left.

At this instant I am half strength. Half of me is here with Keshav, but half lurches with panic at the thought of Shankar alone and unconscious and starving for oxygen. Keshav isn't beside him. Neither am I.

He'll be safe. Masud is coming for him. Focus here.

I blink and shake my head and clutch the matchbox tight.

Jaggu brings the next match down.

Masud is coming. The dogs have found their way back to him, but they are hot and exhilarated, tails restless, tongues out. They make disorderly circuits and shout challenges at trees and shadows. Masud doesn't like knowing what they have done. It makes him feel the dogs are no better than the men, the only difference that they're on his side. One of the first to catch up with them carries in her teeth the bloody, frayed wallet. She drops it on the road a few feet ahead of him and waits, tail swinging. Masud doesn't pick it up.

Masud decides his first priority is getting this girl to safety. They will follow the train tracks if need be to Amritsar, or else to the nearest station where he can put her on a bus to her relatives. Maybe at the station he can place her in the care of a decent-looking family. He still has some money in his black bag, sewn by hand into the lining years ago, just in case. More than enough for a fare. Masud, at this point, still thinks he can part with her. He has gone his whole life without a daughter or a wife. He cannot imagine the intensity of what he is about to feel, the love that will free his tongue.

When he sees my son just outside the village, unconscious beside the road, his reflexes take over. Simran watches him fix the stethoscope in his ears, then, because it seems right, she, too, kneels beside Shankar. She lays her hand on his head, lets it run through his sweat-damp hair. He reminds her of her little brother, Jasbir.

Masud's mouth has fallen open. He hears two things. One he thinks of clinically. A total absence of breath sounds over the left chest. Pneumothorax. Emergency. Move.

Under that alarming silence pulses the gush and whistle-click of Shankar's heart. It is so unusual, the defect so vanishingly rare, that Masud's meticulous medical memory has treasured its music for years. He leans over Shankar's face and nods even as he unwraps the sterile needle and syringe. *I remember you, little one. I have listened to your heart before.*

.   .   .

The second match snuffs as it strikes. The third. His friends are watching him. He is getting impatient. He has handled the matches all night and hasn't had this much trouble. Did they get wet? No, they wouldn't flare like that if they were wet. He is puzzled. He strikes a fourth match. I keep my hand in place, staring at the stubble on his cheek, the absurd tilak on his forehead. I can imagine the perfunctory shlokas, the tugged earlobes, the circular shake of the bell that preceded this expedition.

The ring of men around Keshav shifts a little and breaks. The one named Mangal comes over to see what's wrong. He has his hand in his pocket; he has a matchbox of his own. This one has a Devi printed on it, Gayatri, riding a tiger. It is a simple line drawing. Her arms hold a discus, a mace, a conch shell. The fourth hand is held flat, a red dot on the palm, blessing.

Run, Keshav! This is your chance!

If only I could tell him there's an opening behind him he can slip through. It's such a miraculous device, a voice. I never knew how miraculous when I had one. A radius of disturbance that originated in me and signified something. I don't have a voice. I open my mouth and jut my face forward, but nothing comes out. Keshav is looking from one man to the other. I lunge as Mangal takes out a match of his own and aligns it to strike. A quick bob of his hand, a practice stroke.

Part of the lawyer's roof cracks behind the wall. Sparks fountain into the night sky and glide over the treetops, over the wall, over us. The smaller ones blink out while still airborne, shredded feathers of ash. The larger ones arc and float and loop and fall on us, still lit. Keshav stands under them, staring up. I split myself a third time and leap into the sky, trying to intercept the sparks with my bare chest. I snuff them in the transparent silhouette of my absence. I see one coming in from the side, and I divide again. Fainter and fainter each time. I have never spread myself so recklessly before. I start losing control of it. I smear into a dome, hints of faces and elbows and twisted torsos deforming my surface. And this dome starts to swell, rise, spread, thinner than dead skin.

The sparks, as they penetrate my chest, swell and brighten like meteors entering an atmosphere.

What Masud has to do now he has done only three times before in his career. It's an emergency procedure, not for the kind of patients who walked, or were carried, into his clinic. Army medics had more practice with the desperate stab and pull, gunfire close by. Masud performed all three of his needle decompressions on a single day twenty-two years ago, after a small earthquake in southern Gurdaspur. The bodies had been crushed by rubble, and his fingers, feeling for the space between the ribs, had dimpled their chests visibly, every strut and rafter snapped. All three patients (only one had been a child) had died by nightfall of that injury and others. And in Gurdaspur he'd had the right supplies, and had been able to leave in a tube.

This child's injuries are less severe, Masud can see, after a quick slide of his scalpel slits the silk. The boy is drawing long, fierce breaths, the diaphragm still pulling though the mind has gone slack. The bruise covers his side, but the ribcage doesn't sink or buckle when Masud's fingertip finds the groove between ribs. The other hand holds the glass syringe clear, its plunger all the way down. He must make sure it doesn't touch anything. Now he reaches in the bag, and his hand comes up already unscrewing, with a deft thumb, the cap of a new iodine bottle. He pours it over Shankar's chest, not rationing it. The Krishna blue of his cyanosis darkens further from the spill of iodine. Masud tilts the needle towards Shankar's collarbone and eases it in just above the heart. It is a risk, he knows—the heart may have grown large, after so many years of the blue disease—but any higher and he risks hitting the vessels under the collarbone. There is only so much room in a chest with a heart as big as Shankar's, but he is counting on the tension of the air to have shifted the heart slightly to the right. Seeing the needle's tip slide through the skin, Simran gasps. The wound on her own chest, at almost the same spot, oozes afresh and spots the gauze square Masud has taped there. Shankar lies motionless, not present to experience the pain. There. It's in. Masud steadies the syringe, steadies his dyed-purple fingertips on the plunger. He draws back.

Now, Keshav, while they aren't looking, go!
I don't have a voice. I barely even have the after-image of a body. Keshav can't hear me. But when he runs, it feels to me like

he has. I sense him sprint through the thin, invisible film that's left of me, popping me like a bubble. I sink in synchrony with the sparks. They turn to ash flakes. I land without troubling the dust. Amar, Jaggu and two others run after Keshav, and their feet pound through me. It is all I can do to follow Keshav where his running takes him.

He starts out headed for Shankar, but he shifts direction quickly. The last thing he wants is these men finding his brother. So he cuts between two mud houses and skips over an open gutter, its long, man-made ditch overgrown with tall grasses.

As his brother, unknown to him, starts to breathe a little more easily, Keshav, too, feels a change. He takes in lungfuls of dry night air, and no matter how hard he runs, he doesn't get short of breath.

Shankar's shortness of breath seems mysteriously transferred to the men chasing Keshav. Part of me knows it's really their dozens of bidis a day, and their soft, well-fed bellies, and the fact that they don't care enough about burning Keshav to chase him very long. Even the paraffin had been only a quarter-can, left over from the lawyer's house, not enough to burn anything but a child. An amusement had presented itself, worth pursuing so long as it was convenient. To sniff the wind and go pouncing on rustles would ruin their night out. I know all this, but I like to imagine Shankar has distributed his suffering to them when, breathless after forty feet, they give up, heads down, hands on their hips. Jaggu, the biggest smoker, gives up first. The others stop running as soon as they see him hang his arms and heave in place. They were looking for an excuse. He bares his teeth, scrapes phlegm from deep in his throat, and spits.

'Matches,' he grunts. They walk back to the burning house, where a dance has broken out in the firelight, their buddies, arms high and index fingers up, shrugging their shoulders and singing. Amar snatches up the fuel can he just emptied and drums on it, sharp and loud and hollow, striking it with his wedding band.

I move away from their festivities. I feel so heavy, I check for footprints. I make my way to Shankar. Simran is staring at Masud, who has Shankar in his lap. The syringe full of air and pinkish froth he has tossed into the brush, and the spot on Shankar's chest is dressed. She is thinking about what Masud just said to her, the first words he has spoken—clearly, without the stammer. As if she were a child, or a woman as trustworthy as a child. 'We can't leave him alone.'

Many small things in that comment make Simran feel safe. The use of a 'we' that includes her. The addition of another traveller, making her not the only one who clings to this frail old man. There will be someone weaker than she, someone she can take care of, her little brother given back to her. The prospect counteracts the deep-reaching shudder and prickle of neck every time she remembers what happened in the sugarcane field. Every time, and she can't help but think of it every few minutes, it's as if Saif's hand touches her again. The pain from the bite was and is far stronger, but the hand did something worse than hurt. It was the inroad of something animal. The snout of a rooting boar. Nausea lurches inside her.

Masud, of course, means what he says medically. The lung is only partly re-expanded, though Shankar does breathe more easily. The tension has been relieved, as he can tell from the subsiding neck veins—but without a tube to drain the chest, the lung could collapse again. He is worried. What he has done here, though necessary, has been a drastic measure, potentially harmful. As a physician, he wants to see it through. But a stronger bond is already forming. Just the act of cradling Shankar like this—it's not something Masud has done often, for all his years of practice. His patients either wailed in their mothers' laps or were old enough to sit on the examining table by themselves. He never had the leisure to cradle one of them.

Shankar stirs. A dream thought makes his brow flinch. He is conscious again, though fast asleep. Masud rocks a little. For the first time, they notice the distant fire of the lawyer's house and the dancing going on there. Masud looks away. The recovery in his arms takes precedence; he has no time to fear. He has slid a partition around Shankar, Simran and himself, swift and private as a hospital curtain, and the cruel joys of those cruel men are outside it. Simran, too, feels unafraid. It's not the dogs who reassure her, though they do maintain their skittish, erratic orbit. It's Masud himself, gentle and quiet and unshaven. Masud who weighs perhaps no more than she does.

'Doctor ji,' she says, speaking up for the first time. 'My name is Simran. What is your name?'

'Ibrahim.'

Simran, stung, searches Masud's face and frame and clothes for some corroborative sign—anything that will connect him to

Ayub, Qasim and Saif, or to the monstrous Mussulmaans of Sikh history. She searches a long time and finds nothing but an old man cradling a child.

Another boy crosses the barrier effortlessly, unchecked by the dogs, not one growl. His clothes stick to his body, and he smells of pungent paraffin. The long run hasn't winded Keshav. He breathes as calmly as Shankar. The sight of the brother, larger in size but otherwise identical, brings everything back to Masud's keen memory: which books he spread open, and to which illustrations; what Sonia looked like, and how she bore long scars on her arms. He smiles at Keshav, and the first thing out of his mouth is a name.

'Dr Roshan Jaitly,' he says. 'Your father is Dr Roshan Jaitly.'

The sound of my name strengthens me for their journey. Masud has Shankar in his arms, Simran holds Masud's black bag and Keshav's hand. Masud asks Simran where she is bound, and Simran, though part of her feels she has already arrived, says Amritsar. When Masud asks if she has family there, she says nothing, but Masud nods as if she has answered, and he promises to put her on a bus. Her answer comes after a few minutes more of walking in silence. 'My Guru is there.' No one hears her. She isn't certain, afterwards, that she said it aloud.

Simran doesn't think of Amritsar the way she did before. It's not that her faith has weakened. Her faith has come out of her captivity untouched by Saif or any other man. She prayed on Ayub's truck as intensely as she had in the mountains. But it was never God she was seeking in Amritsar. It was people. And Simran has people now. An old Muslim doctor, two little Hindu boys—protectors needing her protection. Masud's talk of a bus to Amritsar makes her anxious, and not just because she's never ridden in one before. A few days ago, she might have thought such an opportunity divine intervention, a miracle, God calling her close. In the grey light before this dawn, though, she wants to stay near Masud. That's where she senses blessedness. The closer she stands to him, the calmer she feels. His plan about the bus . . . does he want to be rid of her? Does he consider the boys, too, a nuisance? Stray dogs and stray people, picked up like burrs. No. It's impossible to imagine such thoughts in him. She wishes there were some way she could be useful to him, show him how capable she is. Not some simpering child but Simran Kaur, a Sikh girl, selfless, tireless, strong. If she could just show him, he would never want to send her away.

She watches him for minutes at a time. His back and neck, mostly, since he walks just ahead of her. But she notices, too, the wrapped foot and the open shoe, and the limp.

'Did you hurt your foot, Doctor ji?'

He looks down at it as if she has brought it to his attention for the first time. 'I should change the dressing.'

'Let me. I can do it.' She looks down at the bag. 'Is everything in here?'

He sits down, gratefully, and lays Shankar across his lap. Shankar's arm drops the way I remember it doing when he was an infant. An old reflex of mine wants to tuck it back. As if aware of what I'm thinking, Simran sets the black bag beside Masud and lifts Shankar's limp arm off the dust. Masud, who has been wearing his stethoscope around his neck to have it at the ready, checks Shankar's breath sounds. I watch his face the way patients used to watch mine. There must be no worsening, at least, because he reaches over Shankar and cups the shoe heel. Simran's eager hands brush his. She takes over, placing the shoe neatly beside the bag and unwrapping Rutherford's dressing, dirt-stained and blood-soaked where exposed, fresh white where the shoe covered it. The skin to either side of the cut is white and raised, dead. Rutherford had inked the outer border of the cellulitis. Masud can see a new blush along his shin. Simran sucks in her breath. Her eyes soften.

Masud almost wants to cover his wound, fearing for her. To bring out compassion, he thinks, so soon after what has happened to her—hasn't he added, in a way, to her suffering? At first he marvels at a woman, and at a woman's resources. Masud has seen this in the mothers of ailing infants. So have I. But gradually he marvels at Simran specifically, as I did at Sonia. Not an abstraction: this woman. This one and no other. The one who watches him snip the dead skin from one edge of the cut, then naturally takes the surgical scissors and cuts the other edge. The one who comes very close to his feet to make sure she avoids the intact skin, who checks his face to make sure she is doing it right and isn't causing him pain. He could have done it more quickly. Probably more safely, too. But he doesn't mind giving her this power over him. She rinses his foot with the disinfectant and dabs it dry with the gauze squares he unwraps for her and lays on his palm for her to take. It is a strange sight to see Masud, until now the deft physician, make himself the assistant to her ministrations. That bony hand a little tray for her. She has watched him dress her own wound earlier that night, and her work is neat, girlishly careful. Neater perhaps than he would have dressed it himself. When she is done, she holds her arms out and receives Shankar, so Masud can fix his shoe and rise. Shankar, handed across, turns his face to Simran's chest. Some distress half-dreamed troubles his brow and opens his mouth, and he looks to me briefly as he did in his infancy, rooting to his mother's breast. He opens his eyes.

When Keshav found Shankar cradled by an old man, and then heard that old man speak my name, his first thought was that his grandfather had come to rescue him. I had never suspected he and Shankar might be curious about my parents, but it does make sense. The twins must have gathered their grandparents were still alive and in the same city. Sonia would not have lied to the boys about that. Over time, they must have daydreamed great things about the grandparents they never met. Wealth, drivers in uniforms, a haveli. Maybe they even thought they were being watched, from a distance, someday to be plucked from their lives and declared heirs, their mother waited on by servants and delivered rose sherbet on a tray.

I realize that I have not wondered, all this time, whether my parents and sisters made it out of Pakistan or not. If I had the strength right now, I would go scanning cities for my relatives. I don't. Besides, if they fled before Sonia did and didn't offer to take her and the boys along, I'm not sure I care to find them. I suspect that may well be what happened.

Keshav's sense of smell has got used to the paraffin on his clothes and hair, but every so often his face turns a certain way, or his hand rises idly to brush at sweat, and he can smell it anew. Chemical, sinister. The terror rushes back. Until this night, he always associated the paraffin smell with his mother's cooking—familiar clicks, followed by the catch of the flame. He wants to be rid of the smell. So he rubs earth on his arms and neck. Clawed-up, gravel-flecked handfuls of it. He works them into his skin as if they were soap, but he can't soak or mask the fuel smell. Unlike Shankar, he still wears the kameez the widow Shanaaz put on him. He peels it up and off, leaves it on the ground, and steps away.

He is still staring at it when he hears Shankar scream his name. He rushes over, and Shankar, terrified, looks from Masud to Simran, Simran to Masud. His fear is understandable—these are two strangers he has never seen before, and his brother is nowhere to be found. Keshav rushes his embrace over Shankar as if his brother were on fire. 'Kaka,' he says, pointing at Masud, meaning 'uncle'—specifically, 'father's brother'. My brother. And then, because he has no other term for her, 'Kaki', meaning 'Simran'. Father's brother's wife.

The twins will keep these names for them, never calling them mother and father. For all my gratitude I am, selfishly, I know, pleased.

Keshav's bare arms, I see in the growing light, have streaks of earth on them in a pattern much like Sonia's scars. Those marked arms hold Shankar, but his brother goes calm only under Masud's stethoscope. Shankar looks down at the bell as it touches his silk shirt. An old memory of trust takes over. Keshav guides him into Masud's arms, and Shankar allows himself to be carried—awake now, and peacefully studying Masud's half-bearded, half-stubbled chin as he stares at the tracks ahead.

The heat that day is worst of the days they have wandered. Shankar and Keshav inherited my light skin, and they are peeling at the shoulders, necks and noses. Keshav is wearing Shankar's green kameez now, at his brother's insistence, but it gives little protection. Half of Shankar's torso wears the bruise, whose colour has evolved into an unusual purplish-gold. Twice he tries to walk on his own, but he goes pale and stumbles. Masud scoops him up again. Shankar may be lighter than Keshav, but he is still a grown child, and Masud can carry him only so far. Before the sun rose, he ignored the sharp, growing ache in the small of his back, and he shifted Shankar's weight as little as possible. By noon, when they have followed the tracks east just short of Atari, Masud feels himself going faint. His arms ache, his back, his cut foot. He can't go on, and he slides with Shankar to the ground. The dogs converge, sniffing and whimpering, and Simran dabs and blows on his wet forehead. Shankar looks up at Masud and touches the side of his face.

'I can walk by myself, Kaka,' he says.

Masud peels his wet shirt off his skin, breathing through his mouth. 'Are you boys thirsty?' He glances at Simran. 'Do you need water?'

This is his way of expressing thirst. He says it as though he can go and find them some. Simran places her small hands between him and the sun, and his clenched eyes relax.

In the shade of her hands, he starts saying things that she has been dreading: he can get her on to a bus. It's a short ride now, here to Amritsar. She can be with her people by evening.

'But you?' she asks. 'The boys?'

'We're going on to Delhi,' says Keshav. 'We have to meet our mother there.' His tone makes it sound like the exact place and time have been arranged already.

Shankar says nothing at first. He glances down and fingers the gauze badge on his chest, tracing its frame of neatly torn surgical tape. 'We'll go with you,' he declares. 'I can walk. Just watch. I'm feeling better.'

Simran bites her lip, thinking he means go with her, to Amritsar; but it becomes clear he means with Masud, into Atari. To arrange for her departure. They are only a few minutes off the tracks, on an unmarked road, when Masud turns to the sound of an engine. Simran cringes; as soon as they got on to the road, she feared exactly that sound, because any truck could be Ayub's.

It isn't a truck, though. It's a passenger bus. Masud waves his arms, sensing, as he has before, a detached kindness guiding the courses and intersections of people, which violent men try to disrupt but succeed in disrupting only for a time.

PARTITIONS

Buses have been running only sporadically that August, their drivers as brave as the people who ride them. The one that Masud waves to a hissing stop is driven by a Sikh named Deepjyot Singh, who twice that week has saved the lives of his riders, or the fraction of his riders who would have been targeted. Both attempted stops had taken place at dusk, both times on the outskirts of Amritsar. Once from a Muslim mob, the second time from a mob of fellow Sikhs, who saw his turban in the driver's window and hadn't even brandished weapons, expecting him to stop and let them inspect his passengers. Both times, Deepjyot had flicked up his headlights, set his wipers on the fastest setting (entirely for effect; he wanted his bus to look like a possessed beast), kicked off his sandals, and smashed the pedal. Both times the mob had scattered like krill before the whale. A few knocks and thumps under the chassis had some passengers gawking out the rear glass to see the bodies, and the rest clapping and whistling. Yet he always refused the flapping rupees his passengers tried to force on him as they got off the bus. It was no feat of bravery, he told them, to recognize cowards.

The bus is at capacity behind him, but he opens the door. Masud holds out the money he has cut from the lining of his black bag. He tries to speak, but the awareness of people watching from the windows defeats him. All he can do is point at Simran and swallow. Keshav comes forward to speak for him, and Simran goes quietly up the steps. She is unsettled to see one of her own, a fellow Sikh—and, from the small pictures taped to the dash, one as devout as she. She fears Deepjyot can see the trespass on her as clearly as boot prints over flowers. Keshav explains how she has come from far away and has walked for hours on an empty stomach, but her people are in Amritsar. The passengers, seeing only her face over the guardrail, pity her and shift in their seats. A man in the second row rises, squeezing the standing passengers that much closer together, and gestures at his seat. Simran looks at these people—city people, strangers—and at the driver nodding, waving away the fare Masud offers him. She skips down the steps and faces Masud. 'You are my people,' she says. She waits. Masud stands rigid, the only movement on him the sweat drop past his ear. Keshav and Shankar step closer to her.

Deepjyot Singh speaks up from his high seat. The roof, he offers, has only two families on it as of the prior stop. 'There's room up there for all four of you.' He waves his hand to include them all. 'The whole family.'

So all four of them, the 'whole family,' climb on to the high perch of the bus roof. Simran, as she guides Shankar into her lap, hears the sound of water being poured. One of the families, in spite of the heat and scarcity, hands her a steel cupful in welcome. When they are settled, Masud raps twice on the roof, and the bus starts up again. Each mouth takes one sip. Masud receives it last and takes his own. They are still exposed to the sun, but the wind makes up for it once the bus gathers speed. Below, Masud's loyal strays criss-cross the dust and exhaust, barking not at the bus itself, but skywards. Not in protest, it seems from their tails, but joy.

PARTITIONS

. . .

She is staying with Masud because she trusts him. Trust keeps her from thinking of Masud as a Muslim, or of the boys as Hindus. It's nothing like love yet, so soon after all that has happened. Rather she treasures them for the rare, chance finds they are. Everyone else is a risk. Her own father had been a risk. Leave Masud and the boys, and she would be alone again, though shoulder to shoulder on a bus. The same as on the roadside. How lucky I am, she thinks. She takes her hair back from the loud, hot wind. She brings it forward and restores, at last, her braid.

And so it comes about that at a Sikh refugee camp outside Amritsar, a Muslim doctor ministers to the wounded and dying. Masud presents himself at the medical tents together with Simran. He introduces her as a nurse, and a nurse she will become, in time, with his training. The first wound she helps heal will be Masud's own. The cut on his foot will heal completely, leaving not even the thin, divisive line of a scar.

The doctors who meet them never guess at Masud's lifelong stammer. When Simran is with him, everything he says, even if not addressed to her, is for her ears. He doesn't need a translator when she is around. The surface of his tongue just isn't as sticky any more. The consonants that used to snag there and thrash in place come out freely, fully winged. It seems to Masud that something mechanical in his voice has fixed and oiled itself at last. In the increasingly rare instances Simran isn't with him seeing patients, though, he's thrown back, and has to hurry out to find Keshav or Shankar. In time, he won't require her presence, his speech letting go of her hand and walking on its own.

The doctors, on that first day, express their worry about what may happen if the camp learns he is a Muslim. The young men pacing the grounds here have lost family members, the doctors warn him. They have lost honour. The phrase the doctors use, portentously, is 'make trouble for you'. Simran and Masud have little doubt what that means. It might be better if he continued east, the doctors suggest, on to Delhi—there was word of a large Muslim camp at Purana Qila, already swelling into the largest in the country. He would be safer there.

Masud shakes his head and says he will serve here. During their time in the camp, he takes the last name Singh. The false identity doesn't trouble him the way it would have just a day before, when he walked in the kafila and answered those who asked him with his given, Muslim name. He knows his caregiving is neither Muslim, nor Sikh, nor Hindu. Or rather it is all three of these. The name, on the man or on the God, is something around it, not of it—thinner than the gloves on his scrubbed hands, and peeled off just as easily.

On the third night, when Shankar can walk on his own, my twins set out again to find their mother. They tell no one. Simran is sleeping. Masud is sleeping. The boys pass a few cookfires. The families around them don't look up, remembering other fires, wilder fires, fires that consumed rather than fed. To either side of them, the tents crest motionless, like waves on a pictured sea. This is the problem with distances over water. Everything seems closer. The edge of this camp, Delhi, reunion. They walk endlessly. It feels like they're walking in a circle, the way people will when they have no landmarks and no roads.

'Are you okay?'

Shankar nods.

It's over half an hour before they see a military jeep, and in it, two dozing soldiers. A boundary of sorts. Probably the far edge of the camp at whatever hour the soldiers put away their playing cards, rested their rifles across their chests, and fell asleep. The border they marked between the camp and the hostile world has already shifted. Cloth tents, groups of bodies huddled against the night, unhitched carts have formed irregular new settlements. The spaces among them are filling in gradually. Beyond them, the boys see the slow, sludged rivers of two kafilas, continually emptying into this vast stagnation. Shankar sees it and begins to sob. Keshav sees a pile of trash near by, one of many dumps at what had been, at dusk, the edge of the camp. He climbs to the top of it and shouts the word 'Ma!', fists clenched, chin at the sky. No one stirs, not even the soldiers. The scene before him doesn't change its thick, clotted shuffle, and the single cloud across the moon doesn't change its sluggish writhe. Twice more he calls to her. His voice disperses. It finds nothing to enter, nothing to echo against. He comes down to join his brother, and they walk back the way they came.

They have walked me to the edge of their lives. I don't follow them back to their new family. They are safe tonight, and they will be safe from here on. But I have one last journey to make, back into Pakistan. I have been gathering strength for it, but the wind of the passage dissolves me further. When I arrive at the well, Sonia is standing on the edge of it. Bare feet on a ring of stone. The moment our twins turn their backs to the journey, her last reluctance eases. I raise a hand, and my fingers swirl up and away, a granularity finer than pollen. I watch her balance on the edge of the well, her arms tilted forward, her face tilted down.

I have kept myself from following her all this time. I could not bear to face this. Now I trace her back to the moment on the train platform, and before that as well. I see her struggling against the man who pulls her away. But then, outside the station, when he turns her to face him, she lays her hands on either side of his face. I know him. Ghulam Sikri, the foreman, whose men had been working a few houses down from ours. The ones who had befriended me. They had built the cabinets in our upstairs room. In a flash I remember the voice of Ramchand Parikh, arguing with his wife. *Nothing like that Dr Jaitly, who lets his wife* ... Ghulam Sikri is telling her he has sent his brother to get the boys at the next station—but she must not board that train. He would have grabbed the boys, too, he says, but he arrived just in time to get to her, he couldn't reach them, they had already boarded.

PARTITIONS

The train has left. He is walking with her arm in his fist. Why she walks, at first, even those few steps with him, the strange reflex that drew her hands to his face in that moment of panic and confusion—understanding those few seconds forces me farther back. Now she pulls against his grip, she screams; he jerks her flush and whispers a threat to leave the boys on the train. Her passivity after that, I can understand. But those first seconds, her hands rising to his face—they force me into the past.

He came to visit the new flat when the twins were four weeks old. He had to see if they were his. Not a word passed between him and Sonia. Keshav was napping, Shankar was inconsolable on Sonia's arm. He stood in the doorway and watched her pace and bob, pace and bob. Shankar's thin mewling paused only to store the next breath. She saw him at last and stopped. The wrap fell away from Shankar's chest and right arm. Glimpsing the baby at last—my baby, not his—Ghulam Sikri felt intense revulsion. I can imagine what Shankar looked like in his eyes. Grey complexion, the skull too large for the body, no baby fat. A kind of monkey-infant, absurdly shaven. Its open mouth pulsing with that small, high-pitched noise. The disappointment dizzied him, and he missed a step on the way downstairs, just catching himself. I can see him there, in the past. He had convinced himself, over that month, that he—younger, more virile than me—*had* to be the father. He expected to look at the twins and see himself. His rights would be undeniable once he held his sons face to face. Sonia would pack their clothes and come away. He had envisioned all of this.

Instead he saw Shankar, our beautiful wastrel. And through Shankar, me.

Yet that hadn't been the last time he had visited. Another afternoon, after tears and arguments, she took him to our inside room while the children cried in their cloth swings. They were back out before the last pushes had swung to a stop. It was a hurried regression, a quick sip of the fond former addiction. Naturally it reopened the need. I face it at last: the sight of them together. The sight of him loafing downstairs, endlessly spinning a coin on the step, signalled with a knock when the twins had gone to sleep. I wonder if the old hushed rumour is true, the one about the Muslim male's superior prowess in bed. Yet when I look at them, there in the past, all I see are two young people making love. They suited each other. Certainly I didn't make for a natural match. Strength mating with beauty: what was I ever but the rich old man with the beautiful young wife? It is an old story. A common story. But I never did think it would be mine.

Ghulam Sikri tried not to look at the twins. He didn't ask about them, either. How he must have hated them. One afternoon, he did look intently at Keshav. It had occurred to him, on the way over, that the sickly twin might be mine, the healthy one, his own. To him it seemed possible, logical really, that his heartier seed might be responsible for the strange difference between Sonia's twins. And yet Keshav looked just as much like me as Shankar.

He and Sonia met only during the first year, when I was still healthy, and she and I were still making love. After I fell ill, they stopped meeting. Probably because I stayed in the flat so much more. My patients saw the padlock at my office so often, most stopped coming to see me. So the few times in the week I did make it there, I had no one to examine but myself. Erratic heartbeat, impossibly high fevers, shortness of breath after a few stairs. My legs and feet swelled. They held the contour of my fingertip when I pressed on them. Sonia's own legs had swollen with pregnancy so recently . . . and there I was, a year later, loosening my laces. When I curled up on the cot and began dying in earnest, they had no opportunity at all.

My constant presence wasn't the only reason. After the funeral—Ghulam Sikri cut the wood and built my Brahmin's pyre himself, to save Sonia money—she stopped allowing him upstairs. Maybe because the boys were getting older. Maybe the guilt hit her hardest after I was gone. Or had the guilt been less while I was around because she could make up for it? Was that why she was always so uncomplaining? Was that why I never had to ring my bell a second time?

And so he waited for days outside her flat, watching, knowing she would have to leave soon. We both kept watch, but really, he was her only protector in that city. She didn't know about either of us. Ghulam Sikri declined two opportunities for paying work in the first week of his vigil. By August no one was building much of anything in anticipation of the coming destruction. If she didn't leave, he decided, he would warn her the city wasn't safe and was soon to be less so. Then, on the last afternoon he was willing to wait, he saw Sonia hurry into the street with the twins.

So he followed her to the train station. More than one friend had told him about the trains—everybody knew, it seemed, except for the crowds on the platforms. Where the trains would be stopped. How many of *our boys* would be waiting. He shoved people aside as he tracked her, always staying close enough to tap her shoulder.

I can go back and pick him out of the crowd, now that I am willing to face this. There he is. He is staring at the twins. The bald spots on opposite sides of their heads. He believes they are the ones who have kept Sonia from him, even in her widowhood, when she should have been his. He had been so overjoyed I was gone, he had spent a whole day in the sun building my pyre. But when he arrived for his reward, the door was locked to him, and he heard the boys, as usual, crying inside.

It's on the platform he conceives the idea. *How easy it would be*, he thinks, *to part them. I could have her for myself at last.* He waits until the crucial moment when her hands release their hands and she is rising, as if on a wave, into the marked train. He has held that braid before, twisted it around his hand as he stood behind her. He reaches for it again, as is his right. He pulls.

For four days, he kept her under lock. On the fourth, she called to him, begged him to find her boys, tugged his hands on to her breasts and pleaded. He led her to the bathroom and filled a bucket and ordered her to wash. The water was icy. Watching her bathe had been one of the things he had never been able to do. He told her he loved her and that out of love he wished to give her a new life. The life they should have had together. With that new life, he would give her new sons as well. Everything would be restored to her, he promised. Just not in the same form.

And then he called her a new name. And then he undressed.

And now she is standing over the well. In her mind, she hears the sermons of her childhood. Warnings about the wages of sin and the evil in woman. She believes her boys are dead and that she, because of her sin, has caused their deaths. She steps into the well. The splash she makes is small. There are other women in the well. Cold arms and cold hair stroke her scarred arms and chest. She is only neck deep. She lowers her face. She kicks to make room for herself. At last, the bodies under her shift and give, and she sinks a little, the part in her hair still visible above the water. It takes a few minutes. Bubbles rest on the surface. At last they break, and she is released. I follow her into the universe.

*

On my last day alive, I asked for a newspaper. I hadn't asked for one in maybe seven months by then. It wasn't an expense I could justify. But on my last day, I wanted one worse than I wanted breath. Sonia took Shankar on her hip and called down the stairs to the boy of ten or so who hung around the flat and ran errands for the tenants. Meanwhile Keshav stood by the cot, pointing at places on my arm and pressing his mouth on them. Sonia had taught him hurt places were to be kissed. I must have seemed all one hurt place. It was a kind of anointing.

My hands had trouble with the paper. Sonia unfolded it for me. I took it from her. I don't know what I was looking for. I think I wanted the feel and smell and crinkle of my old interest in the world, and the simple physical act, too, of holding the world open and reading it. I wanted some of its dark stain on my fingertips again. There were stories about the war, I remember, and what it meant for British rule. Weariness overcame me, and I let my eyes blur the letters. I took in only the various sizes of the headlines. The stories became blocks, bricks of a single edifice I could not enter.

Shankar and Keshav tapped and then grabbed at the paper. What had loomed like a wall warped, shook, crumpled. 'Come, boys, Pappa is reading.' Sonia drew them away. I let the *Times* slide to the floor, still open. 'They can have it,' I said. She let them go, and the twins descended on the newspaper. First they pulled the pages apart. The vast planes of paper were bigger than they were. Shankar put one over his head and let it slide off. Sonia glanced at me and tried to keep the sections in some order, but I said, 'They're playing, let them play.'

So together we watched them and did not forbid the joyful shredding and crushing of politics and opinions and events. The room's window faced east, and even though the morning grew brighter, the room seemed to grow darker. Sonia always kept that curtain drawn because my fever couldn't bear the sun.

'Open the curtain,' I whispered.

She didn't rise at first. 'The light will fall directly on you, Roshan.'

My eyes drifted to the floor. Gradually, to the sound of ripping newspaper, my pupils grew large. They stayed that way even after Sonia slid aside the curtain, and the light touched my open eyes.

Acknowledgements

My family stayed unharmed during Partition. My parents were not born then, and my relatives tell no stories about that time, so whatever I know about it, I read in books.

My biggest debt is to Urvashi Butalia's *The Other Side of Silence* (Duke University, 2000). The discussions of the plight of women, children, and Untouchables during Partition is valuable in itself, but the most important parts for me were the translated first-hand accounts of survivors. One of the book's storytellers, an Untouchable named Maya Rani, appears in this novel as the girl who helps the twins find their way back to the tracks in Chapter 4.

I first encountered the story of Buta Singh in the famous *Freedom at Midnight* by Collins and LaPierre, originally published in 1975. I read about it elsewhere afterwards. Buta Singh was a Sikh farmer at whose feet a Muslim girl, fleeing her attackers, took refuge. Masud and Simran encounter each other in a similar way.

Those are the only direct debts to my reading that I can think of although there are probably others. There were several other books I read bits and pieces of, but I don't remember being struck by them the way I was with those two books. Most of these other books described the politics, not the people; and to me, as a novelist, it's the people that matter.

There is one story about Partition that relates to my family. It has to do with the place from which my family originates, on both sides. The story points out the absurdity of what was going on then. The 'semi-independent' princes of the Raj were allowed to pick which country they wanted to join. (This system set up the problematic situation in Kashmir, where the Hindu ruler joined India though his subjects were largely Muslim.) Junagadh, where my parents were born and grew up, close to the Gir mountains, had a Muslim nawab.

This Muslim nawab's family and our Hindu Brahmin one had been warmly connected in the distant past. A forefather of mine had tutored the young princes, and as a sign of favour, the nawab bestowed upon him a gift of land and the surname 'Majmudar' (not to be confused with Majumdar, a Bengali surname). Before that we had borne the more Brahmin-sounding name 'Vaishnav', meaning 'devotee of Vishnu.'

When Independence came, the nawab chose to join Pakistan even though his territory had no physical connection to Pakistan—it was adjoined by the Indian state of Gujarat on all sides, except where it bordered the Arabian Sea. The Indian Army rolled in; a plebiscite chose India, overwhelmingly, if the numbers are to be trusted; and so, over Pakistan's protests, Junagadh was annexed. To this day, some (Pakistani) maps of Pakistan, I have read, insist on inking a green dot in Gujarat, indicating a Junagadh rightfully theirs.

PARTITIONS

I point this out because I like how it gives my ancestry a duality—a Hindu family whose very name was chosen by a Muslim benefactor, and whose home can be thought of as either Indian or Pakistani, or both.

It's the people that matter: My wife and twin boys. My mother and father. My sister and her family. My in-laws (how lucky am I to get along so well with my in-laws?). I have been born this time inside a charmed circle. My art thrives because their love feeds me.

They are the reasons I could write the book. Publishing the book can't happen without very important people, too. David Lynn, editor of *The Kenyon Review*, sent my name to the literary agent Georges Borchardt in New York. Georges swam through an inundation of my work and chose to represent me—I consider that an honor in itself. Riva Hocherman and Sara Bershtel, editor and publisher respectively at Holt/Metropolitan, along with Juliet Mabey at OneWorld, have been passionate supporters of this book, and I thank them for their enthusiasm and careful editorial attention. Finally, I am grateful to every reader of this book, whoever you are, wherever you are. Your time has been a gift.

Amit Majmudar